ILLUSIONS

"Nameless Detective" Mysteries by

BILL PRONZINI

Illusions
Sentinels
Spadework (*collection*)
Hardcase
Demons
Epitaphs
Quarry
Breakdown
Jackpot
Shackles
Deadfall
Bones
Double (*with Marcia Muller*)
Nightshades
Quicksilver
Casefile (*collection*)
Bindlestiff
Dragonfire
Scattershot
Hoodwink
Labyrinth
Twospot (*with Collin Wilcox*)
Blowback
Undercurrent
The Vanished
The Snatch

ILLUSIONS

A
"Nameless Detective"
Novel

By Bill Pronzini

Carroll & Graf Publishers, Inc.
New York

First Carroll & Graf edition 1997

Carroll & Graf Publishers, Inc.
19 West 21st St., Suite 601
New York, NY 10010-6805

Manufactured in the United States of America

Pronzini, Bill.
Illusions : a "nameless detective" novel / by Bill Pronzini. —
1st Carroll & Graf ed.
p. cm.
ISBN 0-7867-0403-9 (cloth)
I. Title.
PS3566.R67I43 1997
813'.54—dc21

97-4274
CIP

For all the loyal readers
who have helped keep "Nameless" and me
in business for three decades.

ILLUSIONS

1

I HAVE A THING ABOUT FUNERALS.

The entire ritual from start to finish strikes me as senseless. You stand in a mortuary reeking of the perfume of already withering flowers and stare down at a wax dummy in a satin-lined box, a dummy with the vague features of someone you once cared for. You sit in a church or synagogue and listen to well-intentioned but hollow eulogies and a lot of words about mortal troubles ended and everlasting life in the Kingdom of Heaven that have little to do with the departed and everything to do with the living. You stand beside a rectangular hole in the ground, listening to more hollow words, smelling grass and freshly turned earth, and if you're a man like me, what you think about is not the prospect of a blissful eternity but the futility of man's earthly existence, living and dying both.

Some people, the fortunate ones who have an unshakable faith, find comfort in all of this; it gives them hope to honor the dead in a formalized ceremony. But as far as I'm concerned there is a better, less painful, just as hopeful way to pay your respects. One that has nothing to do with perching on a cemetery lawn waiting for an object like a half-formed pod creature to be lowered into a hole and covered up with a mound of dirt. Honoring the dead ought to be a personal and private act, like making love. And it ought not to involve a preoccupation with death but rather a celebration of life, of one person's time on this earth and its interaction with your own—memories of good times shared, days lived with pleasure and purpose.

Kerry says my feelings have to do with mortality itself, that it isn't really funerals I hate but the concept that everyone and everything must eventually cease to exist. She says this gently, without censure; she doesn't care for religious ceremony or ground burial any more than I do. We have a pact: no service of any kind for either of us; cremation and the ashes scattered to the winds. Could be she's right about the way I feel. I've seen too much death over the years, too much waste. It doesn't frighten me, it makes me angry because I can't seem to come to terms with why it has to be that way. Issues without apparent meaning, questions without answers, frustrate me. It's the sort of man I am. It's what makes me good at my work.

So there I stood next to Kerry in the Olivet Memorial Cemetery in Colma, half listening to the minister delivering his graveside incantation, thinking these thoughts and waiting for Eberhardt's remains to finally be planted and the ordeal to be over. And the irony was, for all I believed in honoring the dead privately and through a celebration of life, I couldn't seem to dwell on the good memories of my ex-friend and ex-partner. The way he'd died kept intruding, taking over. And what I felt was anger and frustration.

When I'd first heard of his sudden demise, the shock had been like a physical blow. It couldn't have been suicide; Eberhardt wasn't the kind of man who took his own life. It must've been foul play, or some freak accident. But the circumstances and the police investigation pretty much ruled out any other explanation. It was suicide, all right. And why had I even questioned it? A lot of cops and ex-cops finish themselves off with a bullet, for reasons that all too often involve stress and alcohol. Eating their guns, they call it.

Once I accepted the suicide verdict I not only lost the sense of shock but the feelings of guilt and sadness that had followed it. Friends for thirty-five years and yet I could not seem to feel any grief, any real sense of loss. The fact that he'd killed himself was part of the reason; I've always considered suicide to be cheap and selfish, the ultimate act of cowardice. Another part was our estrangement for the past four years—not one word spoken directly to each other in all that time. Still, I should've felt something more than the dull anger, the nagging frustration, shouldn't I? It was Eberhardt lying down there inside the ornate box fitted into that tight little hole . . . Except that it wasn't. A damn wax dummy. The real Eberhardt, the man who'd once been my closest friend, had been gone physically for three days now and from a place in my heart and gut a lot longer than that.

Morbid thoughts, making me even twitchier, more impatient. Kerry sensed my discomfort, moved closer and linked her arm through mine. "You okay?" she whispered.

"Yeah. More or less."

"It'll be over soon."

I squeezed her hand, thinking: He'd have hated this, same as me. That's another little piece of irony. Born Jewish, lost his faith early on; not just nonreligious but a virtual atheist.

And here he's being buried in a sanctioned nondenominational cemetery in a service presided over by a Lutheran minister from Bobbie Jean's church.

I made an effort to focus on the other mourners. Bobbie Jean standing in a tight little cluster with her two daughters and the married one's husband, Cliff Hoyt. Thin and pale and shrunken inside a loose-fitting black dress that covered all of her except for face and hands, the hands washing each other constantly as if she were trying to rub out a stain. Dry-eyed and in rigid control; she'd done all her grieving in private. Dana Macklin, Eberhardt's ex-wife, remarried to the Stanford professor she'd left Eb for ten years ago and now one of the pillars of Palo Alto society, wearing a moist look of bewilderment. Joe DeFalco, once almost as close to Eberhardt as I was, looking rumpled and as ill at ease as I felt. Jack Logan and a handful of other SFPD old-timers—Eberhardt's cronies from the days when he'd been a detective lieutenant. Barney Rivera, tubby little Barney, popping peppermints on the sly and glancing at his watch the way a man does when he's worried he'll be late for an appointment. He caught my eye, scowled, turned aside. He didn't like me much any more and the feeling was mutual. I'd tried to talk to him shortly after I heard the news; he'd shut me off cold. I knew why and maybe one day I'd confront him about it, get it out into the open. But not today.

Two other men completed the graveside gathering, neither of whom I knew. Cops, probably; or maybe clients Eberhardt had developed over the past four years, or casual drinking buddies. People who cared enough to attend the funeral, but who wouldn't care long or deeply. Eberhardt hadn't made friends easily or been close to more than a handful of persons in his sixty years. Dana, Bobbie Jean, Joe, Barney, Jack Logan, me—that was about all. A loner and a workaholic, at least in the old days. Introspective, oversensitive, stubborn and sometimes inflexible, and given to dark moods . . .

Just like me.

Right. But I had saving qualities he hadn't: drive, a sense of worth and purpose, an intense desire to create order out of chaos. I also had a woman I loved too much to want to hurt, an agency that was reasonably profitable, and a line of work I found fulfilling. And I cared too much about life to want to give it up so easily and cheaply, or to leave so much pain behind.

The minister finally finished speaking. Time, now, for the first small shovelful of dirt to be tossed onto the coffin, Bobbie Jean's last good-bye. I couldn't watch that; I looked away, out over the trees and rolling lawns and jutting monuments. It was a cool, blustery day with a high wind that sent broken clouds rushing inland from the sea. The pale sunlight and the fast movement of the clouds created shadow shapes on the cemetery landscape—an animal running, a tall-masted sailing ship, a gigantic ice cream cone, a zeppelin. Illusions. Like the attitudes we build up toward others and toward ourselves that turn out to be false or distorted, so much vapor and so many tricky shadows.

Why'd you do it, Eb? I thought. Who were you, really?

The homicide inspectors had found a suicide note in the glove compartment of his car. A few words scrawled on a piece of notepaper that explained nothing: *I've had enough. I can't keep hurting anymore. You won't believe it Bobbie Jean but I love you.*

Bobbie Jean's words to me on the phone three days ago explained nothing either. "All I can tell you," she'd said, "is that he was deeply depressed and drinking way too much. No, he never mentioned suicide. He didn't talk about anything that mattered, hadn't in a long time. He wasn't the same man, the man I fell in love with five years ago. The last year or so . . . I was sleeping with a stranger."

A stranger to Bobbie Jean made him twice one to me. The Eberhardt I'd known, or thought I knew, *wasn't* the same man who'd put a .357 Magnum to his chest and blown his heart to shreds. The bottom line was, I hadn't known Eberhardt at all. I'd been surprised when he ended our partnership and our friendship on such a bitter note; surprised that he'd maintained four years of silence; surprised that he'd suddenly broken it by calling my office last week for an unspecified reason; surprised that an apparently moderate drinker had turned into a depressive alcoholic; and surprised that he'd been capable of killing himself. All the surprises added up to one harsh truth: The Eberhardt I'd thought I knew was an illusion created and solidified through a series of misconceptions. Even my reading of his private demons had been false.

More than once I'd tried to imagine the way it'd been for him that last night. Sitting alone in his car at three A.M., in an alley out near Islais Creek—the fifth straight night he'd been there on a futile stakeout to catch a thief who'd been stealing cases of expensive hooch from a liquor distributor's warehouse. Brooding because this was the only job he'd had in over a month and his future prospects were just as bleak. Drinking from a bottle of Jack Daniel's, finishing it, throwing it on the floor where the homicide inspectors found it. Taking out the Magnum, a big, deadly piece he'd bought sometime after opening his own one-man agency. Holding the weapon in his hand, peering at the shape of it in the dark, feeling its coldness, nerving himself. And then instead of putting the muzzle in his mouth the way most of them did—pressing it tightly against his chest and squeezing the trigger. I could visualize all of that with no trouble, but the man who'd done those things had no face. He was all shadow and silhouette, the way Eberhardt would be in my memory from now on.

Kerry moved against me and I realized the burial rite was done; the other mourners were already drifting away. We went too. Ahead I saw Joe DeFalco say something to Barney Rivera, who ignored him and hurried on. Joe stopped, frowning, and when Kerry and I reached him, he fell into step alongside me.

"What the hell's the matter with Barney?" he said. "He acts like the two of us have leprosy."

"You know the answer to that, Joe."

"Yeah. But for Christ's sake, we didn't have a clue Eb was suicidal. Not a clue."

"We might've if I'd returned Barney's calls." Rivera had telephoned my office twice last week.

"You don't know he was calling about Eberhardt. And even if he was, why the hell didn't *he* say something?"

"Maybe he didn't know how bad the situation was, any more than we did."

"Then why blame you and me? We're not miracle workers."

"I didn't return Eb's call either," I reminded him.

"And he told Barney you didn't? Yeah, I suppose. Still, Eb's message to you didn't say why he wanted to talk. Didn't have to be that he was looking for help, somebody to keep him from pulling the trigger on himself."

"Why else, Joe? His message did say it was urgent I contact him by Sunday night. Figures that was his original target date. The fact that it took him another two days to nerve himself up indicates second thoughts."

"Maybe. So why didn't he call me when he didn't hear from you? Or go to Bobbie Jean? Or call the suicide hotline? Why you and nobody else except maybe Barney?"

I had no answer for that. I shook my head.

"Anyhow," DeFalco said, "it's not your fault any more than it's Barney's or mine. You were two hundred and fifty miles away, up to your ass in white supremacists. I wouldn't've returned personal calls either, in your place. I *didn't* get in touch with Eb, for that matter, and I could have. We talked about it on the phone, remember?"

"I remember."

He blew out a heavy breath. "So what about you?"

"What about me?"

"You're not shouldering any blame, are you?"

At first I had, a little. No longer. Even if I had talked to Eberhardt and he'd unloaded on me, what could I have done or said from a distance of two hundred and fifty miles and four bitter years? How can you stop a stranger from acting on a death wish you don't condone and can't really understand?

"No," I said.

"I hope not."

"Let's drop the subject, okay?"

"Sure. Over and done with anyway, the whole sorry business. I don't even know why I put myself through today. I should've stayed home with Nancy." Nancy was his wife. DeFalco's only religion was the newspaper business, but she was a strict Catholic and Catholics consider suicide a cardinal sin.

"We all should've stayed home," I said.

"I can use a drink. How about you? Kerry?"

"Too early for us," she said.

"I know a place in Daly City, not far from here. You can both have mineral water or something. I feel like company."

But I didn't, and it was plain that Kerry felt the same. "Not today, Joe," I said. "We'd only talk about Eberhardt and I've had enough. More than enough."

In the parking lot DeFalco went off to his car, and as Kerry and I neared mine, Dana came over in hesitant strides. We'd exchanged a few words before the church service; it was the first I'd seen her in several years. She looked trim and fit, her face so smooth and unlined I decided she'd had it lifted not too long ago. The good life in Palo Alto. There was a time when I'd resented her for cheating on Eberhardt, breaking up their marriage, but that had been long ago. I wondered now if she'd woken up one morning to find herself lying next to a stranger, the same as Bobbie Jean had, and if that as much as anything else was what had driven her into the professor's arms.

She said tentatively, "I wish there was something I could say."

"Me, too. But there isn't."

"I can't even cry for him. A man I was married to for nearly twenty years."

"You didn't know him anymore, Dana. None of us did."

"Yes, but still . . . I wish I could shed just one tear. You loved him too, once. You know what I mean."

"I know what you mean."

"Well." She produced a pallid smile and said, "Take good care of yourself." The smile shifted to Kerry. "Take good care of each other."

I watched her hurry off, thinking that it was the last time I would ever see her and not feeling anything one way or the other. And a few seconds later Bobbie Jean was there, alone,

Cliff Hoyt and the two daughters looking on solicitously from a short distance away.

I remembered Bobbie Jean as young-looking, active, high-spirited in a controlled way. In the past few years she had aged visibly: a fine tracery of lines and wrinkles marring her facial skin, the brightness leeched out of her blue eyes, her movements stiff and slow like an old woman's. The years themselves weren't responsible, I thought. Eberhardt, the stranger in her bed, and her life with him were to blame.

She said, "Thank you both for being here," in the formal way of speaking people adopt at funerals. Oddly, her South Carolina accent, which she'd all but lost after more than a decade on the West Coast, had become pronounced again. Or maybe it wasn't so odd: a yearning, conscious or unconscious, for home and better days.

"Nothing to thank us for, Bobbie Jean," Kerry said gently.

"I don't know that I'd've come, in your place. After the way we treated you—not going to your wedding, no card or anything. I wanted to accept the invitation, truly, but . . ."

"But Eb didn't," I said. "No part of it or us."

"He still blamed you for what happened to our wedding plans. Stubborn and bitter and carrying a fool's pride. I'd still have married him if he'd asked me again, or I would've until recently. But he never did. I'm so sorry I let him talk me around to his way of seeing things."

"Past history, Bobbie Jean. None of that matters now."

"I just want you to know. So sorry about everything."

"Us, too. You going to be okay?"

"In time. My girls, and Cliff, have been real supportive. I'm staying with Pam and Cliff for the time being. That house, Eb's house . . . I couldn't keep on living there. He willed it to me but it isn't mine, not my home. I can't go back to it."

Kerry said, "Of course, not for a while."

"No, I mean ever. Not even to pick up the rest of my things. Pam will get them for me. I don't want any of the furniture—it can all stay with the house when it sells." She drew a shallow, wincing breath. "Eb's things, his personal belongings, I don't know about those. Cliff and the girls can put them all in boxes and have the Goodwill come for them, but that doesn't seem right. Without somebody sorting through it all first, I mean."

Her eyes were on Kerry, but it was obvious enough what she was leading up to. I said, "No. Not me."

The burned-out eyes slid my way again. I could almost feel them like too-dry fingers moving on my face. "I don't have any right to ask you, I know that, but there's no one else—"

"Barney Rivera."

"He and Eb weren't close. He never once came to the house after the poker game you all had broke up."

"Joe DeFalco then."

"He's not the right person, if he'd even agree to it. And I don't believe he would."

"What makes you think I'm the right person? That I'll agree?"

"You and Eb were such good friends once—"

"Were we? I'm not so sure of that."

"Closer in some ways than he and I were," Bobbie Jean said. "But that's not the only reason. There's more than just his personal things—his business affairs, too. His office files and all. You'd know what to keep, what to throw out. Some of his clients you might want to—"

"I'm not interested in taking on a dead man's clients."

That came out harsher than I'd intended; Bobbie Jean winced again and Kerry's fingers dug into my arm. There was a brief, awkward silence before Bobbie Jean said in a labored voice, "Oh, God, I didn't mean . . . I don't know what I meant. I know how you must feel. I shouldn't be trying to burden you at a time like this. I'll find someone—"

"No, you won't," Kerry said. "You have too much to deal with as it is. We'll take care of it—it's the least we can do."

I threw her a sharp look. She answered it with one in kind. She has greenish chameleon eyes, the sort that change color shades according to her emotions; the darker they get, the more determined she is. They were very dark now, more black than green, jadelike.

"We'll take care of it," she said again, as much to me this time as to Bobbie Jean. "One or both of us."

"Are you sure?"

"Positive."

"The keys to the house and his office are at Pam's . . ."

"Cliff still works in the city, doesn't he? Well, he can drop them off one day next week. Or if he's too busy, we'll pick them up at his office."

"He'll drop them off. Kerry, thank you. Thank you both."

Another wan smile, and Bobbie Jean went slowly to rejoin her family. As soon as she was out of earshot, Kerry said, "Take it out on me, not her."

"What?"

"Your rage at Eberhardt for killing himself. Bobbie Jean doesn't deserve to be hurt any more."

"All right," I said.

"I can't turn my back on her. I don't see how you could."

"I don't want any part of his leavings."

"Fine. Then I'll do the sifting and sorting myself."

"No. No, you won't."

"You just said—"

"I know what I just said. But it's not your place, it's mine. I don't like it, not one damn bit, but I'll do it."

She gave me one of her analytical looks. "You'd have agreed to it eventually on your own, even if I hadn't stepped in, wouldn't you."

"What makes you think that?"

"I know you. Grumble and grouse, get it out of your system, then you're reasonable again. Most times anyway."

"Don't be too sure you know me as well as you think you do."

"Tough guy. Mr. Macho."

"Just set in my ways."

"Mr. Bluster with a heart of cream cheese."

"Get in the car," I said. She went around and got in. I slid under the wheel. We sat there for a little time in the cemetery quiet, not looking at each other. Or at least I didn't look at her until I said, "I'm not doing it just as a favor to Bobbie Jean."

"I know that, too."

"Yeah? Then why else, smartass?"

"You think there might be something in Eb's leavings to explain what made him shoot himself. It bothers you, not having a clear idea. It's why you haven't slept more than a few hours a night since it happened."

Without answering, I leaned forward to start the engine.

"See?" she said. "I do know you just about as well as I think I do."

2

THE REST OF THE WEEKEND WAS LOST time, empty time. And that's another thing I have against funerals—they leave you at loose ends, depressed to one degree or another. Everything seems gray for a while afterward; nothing looks or tastes or feels quite right, as if the loss of a friend or loved one has been made even more acute by your attendance at the ceremonial coverup of the remains. Even the time-honored wake—I've been to a couple of those, too—has the same hollow, dreary effect, at least on me. The gaiety always seems forced, the party atmosphere faintly repellent and disturbing, as though you were taking part in an ancient pagan rite designed to ward off evil spirits.

Kerry and I spent Saturday afternoon and evening at her condo in Diamond Heights. Neither of us felt like going out; but staying in was a monotonous string of gin rummy games, bad TV programs, reading matter that wasn't particularly involving, tasteless food, and careful avoidance of mentioning Eberhardt's name in any context. Shameless, the black-

and-tan kitten we'd adopted, sensed our moods and pretty much left us alone, proving that cats can sometimes be wiser than humans. We went to bed early and made love, and in keeping with the rest of the day, it wasn't very satisfying for either of us. I didn't sleep well again. Kerry was almost as restless in the early-morning hours.

She had a Sunday brunch with one of Bates and Carpenter's out-of-town clients—"one of the many perks," as she put it wryly, "of being Creative Director of a large, aggressive ad agency." So I left her a little before nine and drove to my Pacific Heights flat. A married couple maintaining separate residences has its drawbacks, but for individuals like Kerry and me, who value and require a certain amount of privacy, it's an arrangement that has more plusses than minuses. Most of the time I like her condo, but when she's not there I always feel more like a visitor than a resident. On days such as this one I prefer the old-fashioned, semi-sloppy ambiance of the Laguna Street digs I've leased for nearly three decades.

I hadn't spent much time there lately and the rooms had a musty, closed-in smell. The day was a carbon copy of Saturday, cool and cloudy, so I opened windows in the bedroom, bathroom, and living room bay to air the place out. Then I wandered around trying to find something to occupy both my hands and my mind. Carbon copy of yesterday in that respect, too: nothing appealed, nothing held my interest for more than a few minutes. By noon I was wrapped up hard and tight like an oversize handball, metaphorically bouncing off the walls. I bounced myself out of there finally, into the car and down to Union Street. Sunday crowds made parking all but impossible; both garages where I can usually find space were full. To the Marina then, where I lucked into a curbside spot just off Chestnut. I walked over to Fanucci's and treated myself to a calzone. Fanucci's makes the best Italian sausage calzones in the city, but this one did nothing for my mood; for all the enjoyment I got out of it, it might have been a plain burger from the Mickey D's on Lombard.

After lunch I walked to the Palace of Fine Arts. Clots of noisy tourists drove me away again, back to the car. So then I went driving. Not headed anywhere in particular, just killing time and trying to work through the restless, out-of-sorts mood. That was what I thought at first, anyway. It wasn't until I was down on the Embarcadero, aimed toward the China Basin Bridge and Third Street, that I admitted to myself I'd had a destination all along, drawing me as surely and inexorably as a magnetic field draws particles of iron.

The alley was off Third, between what used to be Army Street—Cesar Chavez Street now—and the Islais Creek Channel. Bolt Street, it was called. Block-and-a-half long, wide enough for two semis to scrape past each other, walled on one side by a truck storage yard behind a cyclone fence topped with coils of barbed wire, on the other by a string of small industrial warehouses. The building stretched across the upper end, creating a cul-de-sac, was bisected into two halves lengthwise; the half that fronted on Bolt Street belonged to the liquor distributors, O'Hanlon Brothers. A long loading dock with three recessed truck bays ran along the facing wall; the dock and all of the bays were empty on this Sunday afternoon. The entire alley was deserted except for a couple of overflowing Dumpsters next to the storage yard. A gusty wind off the Bay nearby played with scraps of litter, swirling them along the uneven pavement, building little heaps in doorways and crannies. In broad daylight Bolt Street had a desolate feel. At 3 A.M. on a cold, dark, foggy morning, it must have seemed like the back end of nowhere.

Halfway into the abbreviated second block, on the right side, I saw the sign for a solenoid valve company. Its entrance was set back about fifteen feet from the street, the open space in front formed by the ends of two shallow concrete docks; the space was long enough and wide enough for two cars parked parallel, three if they were slanted in diagonally. The docks were high enough so that at night the space would be in heavy shadow—a perfect location for a one-man surveillance stakeout.

This was where Eberhardt had been parked last Wednesday morning. This was where he'd blown the hole in his chest and his life out through the exit wound between his shoulder blades.

I pulled in there, sat for a minute, then got out into the chill wind and stood listening to it whistle and moan through the narrow canyon, looking down at the pavement, around at the empty docks and weathered wooden walls and closed doors and dirt-blinded windows. Waiting to feel something—I wasn't sure exactly what. Not an emotion like sadness or sorrow; it was too late for any of that. Morbid curiosity wasn't what had brought me here either. Waiting for some sort of psychic connection, I suppose, as if by standing on the spot where he'd died I could summon up an insight into his reasons why.

Foolish notion.

I felt nothing at all except cold.

Pretty soon I closed myself inside the car again and switched the heater on and then drove ahead to the O'Hanlon Brothers dock and turned around in one of the truck bays. On my way out of Bolt Street I thought that it was easy enough to understand why Eberhardt had picked this place to die in. It wouldn't take much for a despondent, drink-sodden man sitting here night after night, listening to the wind and staring into the foggy dark, to convince himself that this dead-end alley should be his own dead end. A combination of things had brought him to that point—failure, frustration, lost hope, bitterness, the physical erosions of advancing age. But there also had to be a trigger, some occurrence or revelation or final indignity, to make him go through with it. No matter how mired in despair a man might be, he doesn't just all of a sudden trade living for dying. Something prods him across the line between thinking about it and actually doing it. Every suicide, every homicide has its trigger.

What was Eberhardt's? Kerry had been so right—it was what kept bothering me, why I was having trouble sleeping. What had caused the poor sorry son-of-a-bitch to cross the line?

Monday.

I was half an hour late getting to the office, something I seldom allow to happen. For the first time in over a week I'd slept most of a night straight through. A nearly sixty-year-old body like mine can take only so much stress and sleep deprivation, and then it was either release and regenerate or something would give and I'd find myself in the hospital or an ornate box like the one Eberhardt had been planted in. The choice wasn't a conscious one; my body had made it for me. Good old reliable body. So far, anyway.

The night's rest had put me in a better frame of mind. Hardly cheerful, but at least the funeral hangover was gone and I could start a new work week without dragging my butt. One day at a time.

Tamara was busy at her computer when I walked in.

Wearing an all-green outfit today, and a bright green, new-looking jade heart on a gold chain around her neck. In profile and in concentration her dark, round face had a burnished look, as if it were being lighted from within.

Watching her tap away on the Apple keyboard, I marveled again at the change in her in the short time she'd worked as my part-time assistant. When we'd first met she had been hostile, brimming with the protective cynicism too many African Americans develop by the time they reach college age, the result of constant reminders that the biggest damn lie in America is that ours is no longer a racist society; and her attitude toward the "private eye business" had been one of scornful amusement. Computer hacking was all she cared about; the job with me was nothing more than a way to earn expense money while she pursued a computer science degree at San Francisco State—drudge work, like clerking in a store. But the much-maligned private eye business can be seductive. It isn't glamorous or exciting, at least not ninety-five percent of the time, but it is challenging; and doing it properly requires intelligence, ingenuity, initiative, and skill at problem-solving. Once Ms. Corbin discovered these truths, her attitude began to change, and before long she'd become a passionate convert. In the past six months she'd dragged me forcibly into the computer age by refining all phases of my "retro operation," to the point where she was doing a third of the work on her PowerBook in only twenty hours a week and thus rapidly becoming indispensible. If she quit on me today I'd be in a hell of a bind. As an unrepentent technophobe, who wouldn't know a megabyte from a dog bite, I could not even get into my own files without the aid of someone who was above average in computer literacy. Not much chance of Tamara quitting, though, not for a while yet. She was so thoroughly seduced that she'd admitted to the serious consideration of a new career goal: high-tech investigative work.

She finished typing, read over what was on the screen, smiled at the thing as if it had been a good boy, and turned to give me a once-over. "Yo," she said. Then, "You look tired and kind of beat up."

"Thanks so much. Aren't you going to tell me I'm late, too?"

"You're late. Twenty-nine minutes."

"Should we dock my pay?"

I said that jokingly, but she didn't smile. She said, "Pretty rough, huh? The weekend?"

"Not one of the best."

"That man Eberhardt's funeral?"

"Yeah. I hate funerals."

"Me, too. I had to go to my grandmother's a couple of years ago. Tore me down for days afterward. You know that book by Jessica Mitford? *The American Way of Death*?"

"I've heard of it."

"She was right on, man. Dying sucks."

"Amen to that." Tamara had made the coffee; I went over to the hot plate to pour myself a cup. "You had a good weekend, at least. Romantic one with Horace."

". . . How'd you know that?"

"Deduced it."

"My boss man, Mr. Sherlock Holmes."

"You're glowing, for one thing. You always have that look after a romantic weekend with Horace. A sort of self-satisfied glow."

"Hell I do," she said, and then laughed. "Okay, maybe so. What else?"

"That jade heart you're wearing. It's new. Horace gave it to you, right?"

"Could be a present from my family. Or could be I bought it for myself."

"It isn't the kind of jewelry you usually wear. And if somebody in your family'd given it to you, chances are you wouldn't be wearing an all-green outfit—also not your usual color—to show it off. Nothing's quite so special as a present from a lover."

"Lawsy, Mistuh Holmes, you sho' is a caution. Yes you *is!*"

"Whenever you do Butterfly McQueen, it means I'm right."

"Mr. Smug. Okay, you're right."

"Special occasion? The jade heart."

"Uh-uh. Man just loves me, that's all."

"You going to marry him one of these days?"

"Sure thing. Day he joins the New York Philharmonic and plays his first gig in Carnegie Hall." Horace was studying to be a concert cellist, so she was only half kidding. "You want to know what I gave him this weekend?"

"No." I took the coffee to my desk. The mail had already arrived, a meager little pile for a Monday. I shuffled through it.

"No checks," Tamara said. "I looked."

"No calls either, I suppose."

"None on the machine. One about fifteen minutes ago."

"Client?"

"Man wants to be. Your kind of job, but you won't like it."

"Why won't I like it?"

"He's looking for his ex-wife. She disappeared three years back in Santa Fe, not too long after they split up. That's where the man lives, in Santa Fe."

"So why does he want a detective in San Francisco?"

"He thinks maybe she's living in this area now. Patterson agency in Santa Fe gave him a list of six investigators here. We were number two."

"Which probably means number one turned him down."

"Uh-huh. But we're hungrier and we try harder."

"Why does the man want to find his ex-wife after three years?"

"That's the part you won't like. Also the part that'll make you take the job."

"It's too early for riddles—"

"Paradoxes."

"Whatever. Talk to me in plain English."

"Better hear the details from the man himself. His name's Erskine, he's coming in at ten-thirty. I figured that'd be okay since there's nothing else on the calendar."

"And when he tells me his troubles, I won't like them but I'll take the job anyway."

"Right."

"What makes you think so?"

"Not the kind of case you can turn down. Bet you five bucks."

"No bet. Why is it women all think they know me so well?"

"Could be you're easier to read than most guys."

"Like a trashy paperback?"

Tamara laughed. "Easy to read doesn't mean there's no substance. Walter Mosley's easy to read. So's Mr. Hemingway."

And James Joyce is hard to read. And so's Mr. Eberhardt. "Hemingway blew his head off with a shotgun," I said, and then wondered what had prompted me to say it. Because Eberhardt blew his heart apart with a .357 Magnum? No connection, no point.

"What's your point?" Tamara the Mindreader asked.

I sighed. "None. No point at all."

She said, "Too early for paradoxes, huh?," and gave her attention to her trusty PowerBook.

3

IRA ERSKINE WAS NOT WHAT I'D expected. He was younger, for one thing—no more than thirty-five. And well turned out and prosperous-looking in an expensive silvery gray Brioni suit and a hand-painted silk tie. Short dark hair and a neatly groomed mustache were both frost-edged with premature gray. He had the look and confident carriage of a successful businessman, which is what he admitted to being: he owned what he termed "a small but forceful financial consultancy firm" in Santa Fe. You might have taken him for a satisfied, complacent man, the kind people refer to admiringly as pillars of the community and who are often approached to run for political office, if it weren't for his eyes.

The eyes were gray, direct; he locked them onto mine and maintained the contact the entire time we talked. But the thing about them was that they were almost scintillant with strong emotion, the dominant one being pain. I could feel his hurt as well as see it, as though he were emitting little pulsing waves of radiant energy. It made me both sympathetic and uncomfortable. Emotion that naked is never easy to face, particularly when you have empathic tendencies as overly developed as mine.

He was packing a load of woe, all right. The root cause of it was his ex-wife, Janice, but she was no longer the main ingredient. It took him a while to get around to what was currently ripping him up inside, and when he did I felt twice as sympathetic and twice as uncomfortable. Most private investigators attract clients whose problems require little or no emotional involvement; they do the job, get paid, and move on unaffected to the next. Not me. All too often I get the bleeders, men and women with such intense personal predicaments that I can't seem to avoid being sucked in to the point of bleeding right along with them. And maybe carrying around a scab or two myself afterward.

Erskine had accepted a cup of coffee when he arrived; he'd also asked if he could smoke, and when I said I'd prefer he didn't, he'd accepted that without argument or smoker's belligerence, even though it was obvious he needed the nicotine. Instead he'd swallowed two cups of black coffee, the caffeine acting as a partial substitute, and asked for a third. That one he nursed, sitting with both hands wrapped tightly around the mug as if he were taking in the bitter warmth by osmosis.

His posture was both relaxed and tense, the way a man who is normally at ease in any social or business situation sits when dark things are warring inside him. He didn't shift position once during our conversation. Or glance once at the voice-activated tape recorder whirring away on my desk. I'd taken to taping all interviews and telephone exchanges, one of the many good suggestions Tamara had made, and while most clients didn't object, they were aware of the recorder and would look at it nervously or suspiciously now and then, as if it might somehow be altering their words or taking them out of context. A few inadvertently altered the pitch of their voices or phrased things in more self-conscious ways once the machine started running, but Erskine didn't seem to be affected that way either.

"Janice and I met at a fund-raiser for the Museum of Indian Arts and Culture eight years ago," he said. His tone was tender, almost reverent, whenever he spoke her name. "From the moment I saw her I knew she was the woman I wanted to spend the rest of my life with. Love at first sight . . . I'd always considered it a ridiculous concept. But it isn't, it really isn't."

I remembered my reaction to Kerry the first night we'd met. "I know."

"We were married after three months. The first year . . . I can't describe how wonderful it was. Janice was working at the Salishan Gallery when we met, but of course there was no need for that after our marriage. She'd always wanted to be an artist, had done some oil and acrylic painting in her spare time. With my support she was able to paint full time. She is, or was, quite good. A very distinctive style and vision. She had two showings while we were together, the second at the Salishan. I think if she hadn't gone off the beam, she would've honed and refined her talent. Become quite successful in her own right."

"How do you mean, 'gone off the beam'?"

"Drugs," Erskine said sadly. "Curse of our times."

"Hard drugs?"

"Cocaine. It started after Thomas was born . . . our son, Tommy. She had a very difficult, very painful pregnancy. Tommy was born Caesarean and there were complications. She couldn't have another child. The combination of that and the pain . . . I suppose that's why she turned to drugs. She seemed to stop caring. Not that she stopped loving Tommy or me, at least not at first. It was a loss of passion, of zest, rather than of love."

"Her zest for everything, including her painting?"

"Yes. After I found out about the drugs . . . she never completed another canvas, as far as I know."

"When was that? That you found out?"

"Tommy was about a year old. I knew something was seriously wrong, but drugs . . . well, that never occurred to me. She'd never used them before. And she was careful to hide her addiction from me and our friends."

"How did you discover it?"

"By accident. A packet of cocaine hidden in her studio. I was looking at some of her older canvases, admiring them, and there it was. I confronted her and she admitted she was hooked."

"And then?"

"I convinced her to enter a rehab center," Erskine said. "She was there six weeks, but it did no good. She was using cocaine again a week after her release and she no longer bothered to hide the fact. She went downhill rapidly. Neglected Tommy. Began staying out half the night. Then she disappeared for three days. I was frantic, I thought something had happened to her. When she finally did come home . . . well, she'd been in Taos with a man, another addict. No shame or remorse when she confessed it to me. That was the final straw. I couldn't keep on forgiving her, watching her destroy herself, colluding in her destruction. For Tommy's sake I filed for divorce."

"How did she take it?"

"She didn't seem to care. Didn't contest it or my claim for custody of the boy. Drugs and money were all that seemed to matter to her by then. After she moved out of our home she lived in an apartment downtown, near the Plaza. Then, three months later, she disappeared completely."

"Before the divorce was final?"

"Yes. She already had the settlement we'd agreed on."

"You let her have it early? The entire amount?"

"She insisted on it and I was afraid not to comply. Afraid she'd do something crazy. I couldn't stand to see her suffer, even then. In spite of everything, I loved her. Even now, after three years, I still love her. I know that sounds foolish—"

"No, Mr. Erskine. Love is pretty hard to kill sometimes."

"Yes. Yes, it is."

"How long had she had the settlement when she disappeared?"

"Nearly three months. I gave her the money when the papers were filed."

"Then what prompted her to leave Santa Fe so suddenly?"

"I don't know. There was no reason I could find."

"Just there one day, gone the next?"

"That's right."

"Cleaned out her apartment or were her belongings still there?"

"She took some things with her. Not everything."

"Any idea where she went?"

"To Albuquerque. From there . . . no."

"How do you know she went to Albuquerque?"

"I hired a private detective to look for her. I couldn't bear not knowing if she was all right. He traced her to Albuquerque but lost the trail there."

"Did she contact you at any time after that?"

"No. Not a word in three years."

"Your son? A birthday card or present?"

"Nothing," Erskine said. "I kept hoping. Trying to make myself believe she'd find a way off drugs, turn her life around, and then . . . if not come back to Tommy and me, at least let me know she was all right. After a year or so . . . I thought she must be dead. An overdose or something like that."

"But now you think she's alive."

"I don't think it, I know it. Alive and recovering."

"What changed your mind?"

"A postcard. A blessed postcard."

"Sent to you or someone you know?"

"An old friend of Janice's in Santa Fe. She received it two days ago."

"Written by your ex-wife?"

"Yes. And postmarked San Francisco."

"Arrived out of the blue?"

"That's right."

"Saying what?"

"I can quote the message verbatim," he said. " 'I'll bet you thought you'd never hear from me again. Tell Ira and Tommy I still love them. Tell them I'm okay now and sorry for all the pain I've caused them.' "

"That's all? No indication of where she might be living?"

"No. It could be anywhere in this area."

"Unless she mailed the card en route to somewhere else."

"No," he said, "no, she's here in northern California. I know it. I can feel it."

"Why do you suppose she sent the card to the woman friend and not to you?"

"I don't know. Guilt, maybe."

"She could be gearing up to send you one, too."

"It's possible, but I can't just wait and do nothing."

"Are you sure the handwriting on the card is hers?"

"No doubt of it. Janice wrote it, and thank God she did. It couldn't have come at a more necessary time."

"Necessary, Mr. Erskine?"

"Because of Tommy. That's why I'm so desperate to find her, as fast as humanly possible. Because of our son."

"I don't understand. Is something wrong with the boy?"

The radiant pain in Erskine's eyes was so intense I had to look away from it. "He has leukemia. The doctors . . . they give him no more than a few months to live."

There is nothing you can say to a statement like that that doesn't sound lame or inadequate. A simple "I'm sorry" comes closest to to being adequate, so I said the words and then we both sat there in heavy silence and waited for enough time to pass so we could get on with the interview. Across the office Tamara was very busy at her Apple PowerBook, pretending not to listen. Ms. Corbin, I thought, I ought to kick you in the pants for letting me get hammered like this.

Erskine finally broke the silence. "They told me a little over a week ago. The boy'd been ill . . . they gave him a battery of tests . . . there's nothing they can do. Janice is his mother, she has a right to know. To see him, be with him before it's over. Even as terrible a mother as she's been, I couldn't deny her that right even if I wanted to. And I don't want to."

Nothing much you can say to that either. I kept my mouth shut.

"Funny, isn't it?" Erskine said, but he was talking to himself, not to me. "The Lord giveth and the Lord taketh away. I'm going to lose Tommy, but maybe . . ."

False hope, even after three years. I cleared my throat before I said, "Did you bring a photo of your ex-wife, Mr. Erskine?"

"Yes. I brought several." He took an envelope from his coat pocket, slid it across my desk. "Keep whichever ones you like. I have the negatives."

There were a dozen or so photographs, a mix of professional studio shots and candid snaps, all in color. Most were head-and-shoulders and full-body poses of a woman alone. One was of her cradling an infant in her arms—the boy Tommy, I supposed. Two others were relative close-ups of oil paintings, one hanging on a wall, the other propped on an easel.

Janice Erskine had been in her mid to late twenties when the photos were taken. She was an ash blonde, slender, narrow-hipped. Eyes green or maybe hazel. Strikingly attractive, though her nose was too flat and her ears too large for the *Vogue* model and movie star kind of beauty. Her mouth was her best feature: wide, well shaped, so that her smile was fairly dazzling. There were no signs of the ravages of drug abuse in any of the pictures; they'd probably been taken early in their marriage.

"Beautiful, isn't she?" Erskine said with that near-reverence in his voice. "Back then she was the most stunningly beautiful woman I'd ever seen."

I said "Yes" and let it go at that. "I take it those are her paintings in the other two snaps?"

He nodded. "I suppose it's a small hope that she has started painting and displaying her work again. No one in Santa Fe has heard any more of her since she left. But I didn't want to overlook any possibility."

I studied the two snaps. He'd said that her style and vision were unique; I don't know much about art, but even I could see that it hadn't been just pride talking. Both paintings—one of an old church stark against a sky full of thunderheads, the other of an age-wrinkled Native American seated on a bench—were so realistic and finely detailed that they approximated photographs. There was no color in either; they were done in primary black, white, and silver, without shading of any kind. The effect was impressive, made even more so by clearly defined lines and angles and the minute detailing.

"Is all of her work like this?" I asked. "No color and no shading?"

"Yes. Janice saw all her subjects in terms of black and white. She said color spoiled the true essence of objects and people. Remarkably talented, wasn't she?"

I agreed that she was.

He said, "Such a shame, a waste to have thrown it all away," which was exactly what I was thinking.

"Is there anything else you can tell me, Mr. Erskine, that might help me find her? Did she have any hobbies, for instance?"

"No, no hobbies. Art was her only real interest."

"Places she frequented, special events she attended?"

"None that weren't art-related."

"Did she have a favorite charity? Do any charity work?"

"Museum and gallery fund-raisers. And early in our marriage, she helped organize a Cancer Society benefit."

"Was she politically active?"

"No. Apolitical."

"Did she ever live in California? Spend much time here?"

"I don't think so. She was born in Chicago, grew up there, and moved to Santa Fe when she was nineteen. It was the art scene that drew her."

"Any visits to this area, with or without you?"

"Not before her fall from grace," Erskine said. "At least none I ever found out about."

Fall from grace. Odd phrasing. But he seemed unaware of

it; his pained eyes had a squeezed, remote look, as if he were seeing or trying to see something deep in the past. So I let the remark ride, waited until his gaze cleared and focused on me again.

"Did she know anyone, even a casual acquaintance, who lived in northern California?"

"No, no one I know of."

"Are either or both of her parents still living?"

"Both dead more than ten years now."

"Other relatives?"

"None. Janice was an only child."

"What was her maiden name?"

"Durian. D-u-r-i-a-n."

"Did she start using it again when you filed for divorce? Or was she still going by Erskine when she disappeared?"

He sighed. "Durian," he said, as if the fact distressed him.

"She may or may not still be using it. Depends on what she's doing now, whether she's in fact clean again and how much connection she still feels to her past. The postcard would seem to be a positive sign. Then again, it could've been no more than a momentary attack of conscience."

"I'm afraid that's all it was," he said. "If she were thinking of coming back to us, or making amends in some way, I'd have heard from her directly by now. Too much time has gone by . . . the only way is for me to go to her."

"And if a meeting should happen? What do you think her reaction will be?"

"Reaction? To me?"

"To the news about your son."

"She'll come back then. She has to."

"Her maternal feelings can't be particularly strong," I said, "or she'd have made some effort to see the boy by now. Did she want a child in the first place?"

That seemed to stir him to the edge of anger. "Of course she wanted him. We both wanted a child, our own child."

"And yet she was an unfit mother—"

"I didn't say that. I said she neglected Tommy. That isn't the same thing at all. It was the drugs. She wasn't herself, she wasn't the same person who . . . It was the goddamn drugs!"

"Easy, Mr. Erskine. I'm on your side here."

He stared at me blankly for a few seconds. Then he seemed to shake himself; rubbed a hand over his face as if wiping away the sudden irritation. "I'm sorry," he said, "it's just that the way I feel about her, even now . . ."

"You don't need to apologize or explain. I understand."

"Do you? I hope you do."

"How long are you planning to stay in San Francisco?"

"How long? Until you find Janice."

"That could take some time, and it might not happen at all. Frankly, given the circumstances of her disappearance, the time factor, and the lack of any definite leads, the odds are against it."

"You'll find her," he said. "You have to."

"Why wait around while I try? Don't you want to be with your son?"

"Of course I do. But he's in the hospital, he has the best of care, there's nothing I can do . . ." Erskine broke off, scrubbed his face again. "You're right. I know you're right. I should go back to Santa Fe, and I will. But not just yet. A day or two . . . I'm at the St. Francis. You can reach me there any time, day or night."

I didn't argue with him; it wasn't my place to tell anybody how to deal with the tragedies in their lives. I had him sign one of the standard agency contract forms, accepted a five-hundred-dollar retainer—he insisted on paying with hundred-dollar traveler's checks—and told him I'd get to work right away. When he left, his shoulders were a little rounded and there was sweat on his neck that hadn't been there before he opened himself up to me.

After he was gone, Tamara said, "Told you you'd take the job."

"Yeah. You should've told me about his son, too."

"Better you heard it from him, wasn't it?"

"Wrong, Ms. Corbin. I don't like being blindsided, emotionally or any other way. From now on I want any and all details up front."

"Okay." She asked then, "What'd you think of the man? Kind of strange, if you ask me."

"Strange? How so?"

"Seems to care more about his ex-wife, woman who hurt him bad, woman he hasn't seen in three years, than about his dying kid."

"He's torn up inside. Pain has different effects on different people, you know that."

"I know it. Boy'll be gone pretty soon and there's nothing he can do about that, but she's still alive. So he figures maybe he can talk her into coming back to him, sharing the grief."

"Seems to be what's in his head."

" 'The Lord giveth and the Lord taketh away.' Uh-huh."

"Don't be cynical. It happens. Probably won't in this case, even if we can find Janice Durian, but if Erskine believes it and it helps him get through, what's the harm?"

"No harm, no foul," Tamara said and shrugged. "But I still think he's a strange dude."

4

SKIP-TRACING CAN BE EASY OR IT CAN be difficult as hell, depending on the person you're trying to find, how much detailed information you have, how long he or she has been missing, and how much effort the individual has put into covering past tracks and/or in building a new life. Three years is a long time, but I'd once located a man who had taken considerable pains to remain hidden under another name for a full decade. And I'd done it, with the aid of a little luck, in less than a week.

The thing is, it's pretty hard in the society we live in to drop out of sight and keep on functioning without leaving a paper trail. You can change your identity, your means of earning a living, your habits, but unless you become one of the faceless soldiers in the traveling army of the homeless, the new identity still builds a paper trail that can lead straight to your door. In my dinosaur days—a woman at the state board of worker's compensation had referred to me in those terms, not long ago, when I'd told her I didn't own or know how to operate a computer—I'd conducted my skip-traces by personal interviews and document searches and by telephone through contacts at various city, state, and federal agencies. Now, thanks to my good sense in hiring Tamara and her hacking skills, I let her handle most of the paper-trailing and then do whatever follow-up legwork is necessary myself. She has instant access to all sorts of information that would have taken me long hours, even days, to gather. As a result, most skip-traces are simpler and faster to manage, with a higher success rate. The same is true with the bulk of my other cases—personal background checks, suspected insurance fraud, adoption searches, that sort of thing. With the two of us working together, we could handle a third more investigations per month than I'd been able to do alone. We could, that is, if we were able to get the work. The competition in the private detection racket, like the competition in so many other businesses these days, is fairly cutthroat, and it's the big agencies that wield the sharpest knives. Eberhardt wasn't the only one who'd found that out with a vengeance.

The Janice Durian Erskine trace didn't look promising in the early stages. No apparent paper trail for Tamara to tap into. No driver's license, credit cards or credit rating, bank acccounts, or Social Security number under the names Janice or J. Durian, Janice or J. Erskine. The American Cancer Society had no record of her. She also had no local, state, or federal record of criminal arrest, nor so much as a parking ticket, under either name. Which was mildly encouraging in one sense. It indicated she might in fact have managed to overcome her drug addiction. On the other hand, it might also have meant that she'd avoided being picked up on a possession rap or for one of the illegal activities, like prostitution, that junkies drift into to support their habits. It was also possible she'd been arrested and charged under a wholly different name, though most individuals have been fingerprinted for one reason or another these days and a computer check would have turned up her true identity.

Tamara and I contacted each of the various drug abuse treatment centers in the Bay Area. Some refused to give out patients' names; the ones that were willing to cooperate when we explained about Tommy Erskine's terminal leukemia had nothing to tell us.

The postcard indicated Janice Durian Erskine was still alive. But it could've been written by somebody else, despite Erskine's certainty about the handwriting, or penned months or even years ago and just now mailed by someone else for motives of his or her own. So Tamara ran a check on the California death records for the past three years. No listing under either name. Still inconclusive, though. She might have died in another state; and drug addicts often enough perish under circumstances that put them in the morgue as a John or Jane Doe.

Our next step was the art angle. There are dozens of professional arts organizations in San Francisco alone; Tamara and I started with the larger ones—Artwork Marketing and Publishing, Brava for Women in the Arts, the San Francisco Arts Education Foundation—and worked our way down to the small specialty outfits. None of them had ever heard of the subject. Neither had any of the fifteen or so artists' agents operating in the city. That left art galleries, dealers, and consultants, of which there are three full pages in the San Francisco telephone directory; and art schools, art restorers, fine arts artists and commercial artists, which take up another page or so in the directory. And that was just for the city proper. It gave me a headache just thinking about how many more organizations, galleries, schools, and individuals there are in the nine counties that comprise the greater Bay Area, not to mention how many in the entire state of California.

Canvassing the local ones would take days; canvassing them all would take weeks. And Tamara couldn't do it by computer. We'd have to divvy up the San Francisco listings and call each one, with me doing most of the telephone work because she has a full school schedule on Tuesdays; and chances were the effort would net us zero. If there was no paper trail on Janice Durian Erskine, she was probably using another name and therefore not trading on or even mentioning her past affiliation with the Santa Fe art scene. And she didn't have to be living in this area if she was living at all; she could be anywhere in California or one of the other forty-nine states or even in another country. And she didn't have to be working at a job that had anything whatsoever to do with art. Or any legitimate job, if she was still hooked on cocaine.

Anybody who thinks the private eye business is exciting ought to spend a few days sitting in on a problematical skip-trace like this one. They'd be in for a rude awakening. Not to mention a sore head and an even sorer tailbone.

Bobbie Jean's son-in-law, Cliff Hoyt, dropped off the keys to Eberhardt's house and office late Tuesday morning. He was a chubby, usually cheerful man in his thirties—a tax attorney who worked for an old established firm on Montgomery Street. He didn't look particularly chipper when he walked into the agency; his mouth had a glum downturn and his eyes were grave.

"Sorry to be late in getting these to you," he said. "I meant to bring them in yesterday, but I got hung up in court."

"No problem."

"Bobbie Jean really appreciates what you're doing," he said. "So do Pam and I. It can't be an easy chore for you."

I shrugged. "She holding up okay?"

"Not really. She puts on a brave front, but . . . well, it's eating her up inside. I think she blames herself."

"There's nothing she could've done to stop him. Nothing any of us could've done."

"We keep trying to convince her of that," Cliff said. "She says she knows it, but I don't think she accepts it as fact. At some level she feels she failed him—didn't love him enough, didn't give him enough support."

"It's the other way around. He's the one who didn't care enough about her or about himself. And he's the one who pulled the trigger."

"Yes, the ultimate selfish act. Bobbie Jean knows that as well as we do, but knowing it and coming to terms with it are two different things."

"She's strong. She'll be all right."

"Not as strong as she once was. He wore her right down to the nub. She won't cave in, I'm pretty sure of that, and eventually she'll work through it. But it'll take time. And the quicker the closure the better. Her life with him, I mean—severing all the material ties so she can start cutting the emotional ones."

"I'll get the task done as soon as I can, Cliff."

"I don't mean to pressure you—"

"No, no, I understand. I'll try to sort through everything by the first of next week."

"Thanks. For Bobbie Jean's sake," he said. Then he said, "You know, she really does feel bad about shutting you and Kerry out the past four years. Going along with Eberhardt, not challenging or defying him."

"I don't doubt it."

"Pam and I talked to her about it more than once. The harm cutting off old friends can do. But he had such a psychological hold on her. And he grew more and more bitter, more and more screwed up."

"Yeah," I said.

"No hard feelings then?"

"Not toward Bobbie Jean. Never."

"I didn't think so, but I wanted to make sure. I'll tell her again; it might help. Might help, too, if you and Kerry came over to visit at some point. As friends."

"Count on it, Cliff."

He shook my hand. "Let's keep in touch."

"Count on that, too."

Alone, I sat looking at the keys before I put them in my wallet. Two keys that would not only open house and office doors but doors into the past. I had no desire to pass through any of them; to touch any part of Eberhardt now that he was dead and buried. Yet at a visceral level I needed to walk through those doors, for as long as I could stand to be on the other side of them. If any of the missing pieces to his suicide existed, that was where I would find them.

Bobbie Jean needed closure, and like it or not, so did I.

Tamara said, "This phone stuff isn't getting us anywhere. You know what I think?"

"What do you think?"

"There's a better way to find out if there's anything in the art angle. Faster, anyhow. We're just jerking around here, you know what I'm saying? Get it over with and move on."

"Fish or cut bait," I said.

"Huh?"

"An old expression. Means quit jerking around, do what needs doing, move on."

"Sort of like shit or get off the pot."

"You have such a delicate way of phrasing things, Ms. Corbin."

"Hey," she said, "we're private eyes, right? Private eyes have to talk like private eyes, keep up the tradition. You think Bogart said fish or cut bait in *The Maltese Falcon?*"

"No, but he didn't say shit or get off the pot, either."

"Would have if they hadn't had the Hays Office."

"What do you know about the Hays Office?"

"More than you, I'll bet. Like, real name was the Motion Picture Producers and Distributors of America. Man hired to run it in 1922 was Will Hays, former U.S. Postmaster General. Production Code was adopted in 1936. Only about four thousand words long, bunch of generalities in outline form. Paragraph in Subdivision Two, sexual taboos, that says scenes of passion such as excessive and lustful kissing have to be treated so they don't stimulate the lower and baser elements. Code never did define who the lower and baser elements were—"

"Okay, okay. Enough, college girl."

"College woman," she said.

Verbal sparring with Tamara can sometimes be wearying, particularly when it involves trying to build a rickety bridge across the generation gap. And we'd already wasted enough time this Wednesday morning. Almost noon now, and we'd both been on the phones since nine-thirty, turning up one blank after another on Janice Durian Erskine. Diligence often pays off, but on some cases you get certain feelings, and the feeling I had on this one was that we weren't going to find the subject working at any art gallery, organization, school, or other affiliated business in San Francisco or anywhere else in the Bay Area. Any reasonable new tack was fine with me.

I said, "What's your suggestion on the art angle?"

"Well, let's say the woman did clean up her act. Could be she got married again, right? Could be she doesn't need to work. Client told you the only thing she ever cared much about is art, her own painting. So if she did learn to just say no to drugs, got her shit together, what's one of the first things she'd start doing?"

"Painting again. Maybe."

"Maybe's all we got. Say she did. If she's as good as the man says, good enough to have a showing at a fancy Santa Fe gallery, her work's probably still good enough to be hanging in some Salishan clone out here. And from what I know about artists, it'd be the same sort of stuff she used to do—same style, subject matter. You know where I'm coming from?"

"And where you're heading. The thing to do is visit galleries in person, flash the photos of her and her paintings."

"That's it. You're the man."

"Might work. If she's off drugs, if she started painting again, if her work is still good enough to interest a gallery, and if she cares enough and is confident enough to make it available to one."

"No worse odds than playing telephone roulette. Kind of obvious by now she's got herself another name."

"Pretty obvious," I agreed. "So you think I should take those photos and climb on the old shanks' mare—"

"The which?"

"Go out and start making the rounds. Me. Alone."

"Like I said, you're the man."

"Uh-huh. And the man has a better idea. *Two* people can canvass twice as many galleries in the same amount of time."

"Me? Hey, I'm just a hacker and glorified secretary—"

"If that's what you think, then it's time you got out and did some fieldwork. Didn't you tell me you're considering a full-time career in this business?"

"High-tech, high-concept," she said. "Where I'm the boss and my people do the scut work."

"In this low-tech, low-concept agency you're the people and I'm the boss. Besides, the idea was yours. Tell you what. We'll close up now and take those two snapshots of Janice Erskine's paintings down to the fast-photo place on the corner and have them duplicated while you and I eat lunch and decide which of us scut-works where. And then we'll each spend an instructive afternoon in the world of showcase art."

Tamara groaned. Then, slyly, "You buying lunch or do we put it on the expense account?"

"You're learning fast, all right. Too fast. I'll buy."

"Okay. But if I'm the one gets a line on her, how about a reward? Say another twenty bucks a week?"

"So fast, in fact, you'll probably end up owning your own agency before you're thirty."

"I'll settle for ten more a week. Deal?"

"Deal. But only if you get a line on her."

She hopped to her feet, grinning. "Fish or cut bait," she said.

5

It wasn't Tamara who got the line on Janice Durian Erskine; it was me. And it wasn't because the missing woman had begun painting on canvas again, or taken to exhibiting any of her work old or new in a San Francisco gallery. Rather, it was a case of luck and coincidence combined in equal parts—the sort of thing a detective runs into more often than you might think, even on a cold trail, and that can make all the difference between a successful trace and a dead-end one.

The place where I picked up the lead was The Artful Vision, a small but high-class gallery on Pine on the downtown side of Nob Hill. The last one on my list for the day. My watch said a quarter of five when I walked in, and Tamara and I had agreed to meet back at the office at five-thirty to compare notes. I was tired, my feet hurt from all the pavement-pounding and hill-climbing, and I felt put upon and grumpy. In addition to headshakes and verbal negatives, I'd been subjected to down-the-nose sneers and a genteel form of the bum's rush from more than one overdressed, haughty gallery owner or hired help. One glance was enough to tell these snooty types that I probably couldn't afford one of the frames in which their paintings hung, let alone the art itself, and therefore I was not there to buy or even to browse discerningly. When I told them my profession, it pushed their noses further out of joint. A private investigator, to that sort of mind, is a cut above a homeless panhandler, and not a prime cut at that.

There was no one in evidence, haughty or otherwise, when I entered The Artful Vision. But a bell tinkled over the door, so somebody was bound to appear pretty soon. While I waited I looked around at the smallish number of artworks on display—a dozen or so paintings, mostly oils and watercolors of various sizes and subject matters, a few ceramic jars and urns and some metal, stone, and marble sculptures on pedestals. The largest of the sculptures, free-standing, looked to my untrained eye like a go-cart that had hit a wall at forty miles an hour. A brass plate on its base said *Divinity*, which would be enough to scare hell out of you if you thought about it very long. The price, no doubt, would scare hell out of me immediately, though I didn't need to worry about that; The Artful Vision's artful vision was such that it did not insult its clientele by the gauche display of a price tag.

I was peering up at a ten-foot-wide canvas composed of asymmetrical triangles interspersed with blobs, smears, and streaks of off-yellow and pale green, trying to decide if I were just a lowbrow or if it really did look as though the artist had upchucked a plate of succotash, when the woman bustled into view from somewhere at the rear. She was in her forties, stylishly dressed and coiffed, wearing a bright professional smile and a hopeful glint in her eye. The smile slipped a little when she got a good look at me, but she didn't lose it or shift it into a sneer; and the glint also stayed put. I could almost read her mind: I didn't look like a patron of the arts, but you couldn't always tell and I *might* just be one of those eccentric millionaires who take pride in dressing like the common man. You had to keep the faith, after all.

She said, "Hello, I don't believe we've met. I'm Ms. Weissman. That's lovely, isn't it?"

"What is? Oh, the painting."

"Perrault's most impressive work, a genuine triumph."

"Very nice." If you liked secondhand succotash.

"Does it interest you?"

"Actually, I'm not here as a prospective customer."

Her smile slipped a little more at that, and all but vanished when I showed her the photostat of my investigator's license and explained that I was trying to locate a missing woman who had once been a successful artist. The glint dulled and finally winked out. What replaced it was neither coldness nor aloofness, but a kind of resigned neutrality. The kind that permits cooperation, but only up to a point.

"If I can help," she said. "The woman's name?"

"Janice Durian Erskine." I let her have the now well-thumbed set of four photos. "The first two are of her, the last two of her work."

"Her face isn't familiar." Then Ms. Weissman frowned and said, "Erskine, did you say?"

"Janice Durian Erskine."

"You know, that name *is* familiar . . ." She shuffled the snaps and studied the likenesses of the old church and the wrinkled Native American patriarch. "Of course. Silver, black, and white. Southwestern subjects. Janice Erskine."

"You know her?"

"Not her, no. Her work."

"From where?"

"The Salishan Gallery in Santa Fe. As it happens, I was employed there for several months before I moved to San Francisco."

"When was that?"

"Almost two years ago. Twenty-two months, to be exact. I sold one of her paintings while I was at the Salishan—a small acrylic of an Indian pueblo in a rainstorm, if I remember correctly. She had such a wonderfully original style. Utter absence of color, you know, in all of her work."

"So I understand. Were you aware that she dropped out of sight about three years ago?"

"Well, yes, it seems to me I heard something about that. But I don't recall the details."

"They're not important. What is important is that her former husband is eager to locate her because of their young son. The boy is gravely ill."

"Oh, I'm sorry. But I really haven't any idea where she is now."

"There's a chance it may be the Bay Area, which is why I was hired. Tell me this, Ms. Weissman. Have you seen any of her work since you've been out here?"

"Her oils and acrylics? No. No, the only place I've ever seen them is at the Salishan."

The way she phrased that, the question and her inflection, prompted me to ask, "If not oils and acrylics, some other kind of painting that might be hers? Or one that reminded you of her work?"

"Well . . . yes, as a matter of fact. But not a painting. Not art at all, really."

"What, then?"

"A wine label."

". . . You said wine label?"

"That's correct. I know it sounds odd, but my husband

and I were at a dinner party several weeks ago and one of the premium wines the hostess served . . . well, the style of the label reminded me of Janice Erskine's work. At the time, and even more so now that I've looked at these photos."

"A strong similarity?"

"Yes and no. The label was done in silver, black, and white, with lines and angles sharply defined, as in her oils and acrylics. But there was color in the design as well as in the lettering. Vivid blues and greens."

"Even so, in your judgment it could've been done by Janice Erskine. Is that right?"

"I won't swear to it, of course, but yes . . . yes, it could have been."

"What was the name of the winery?"

"Oh, Lord, I don't remember."

"Please try, Ms. Weissman."

She tried. And, "I'm sorry, I simply can't remember. Wines . . . well, I don't know much about them, I'm afraid. All I can tell you is that it was local."

"Local? You mean a California wine?"

"Yes. Napa Valley? That may be it. The woman who hosted the dinner party makes a point of never serving any but local wines. Nothing foreign, you know."

"Would you mind calling her, asking if she can identify the winery?"

She said she wouldn't mind but she couldn't; the woman and her husband were away on a Caribbean cruise.

Minor setback. I thanked her for her help and went out with more energy than I'd had when I walked in.

One of the city's oldest and most exclusive wine shops, the kind that doesn't just sell vineyard produce but offers such other services to the connoisseur as cellar appraisals and wine storage, was a few blocks from The Artful Vision on Sutter Street. A white-haired clerk who might have been a retired sommelier listened to my general description of the label in question, nodded his head judicially, and said, "Silver Creek Cellars. Quite a striking label. Several of our customers have commented on it."

" 'Silver Creek Cellars'. That's the name of the winery?"

"Yes. Rather new, three years or so, but already beginning to make a name for itself."

"Napa Valley?"

"No, no. Alexander Valley. Their estate-bottled cabernet sauvignon and zinfandel are excellent, as robust as any premium reds from that region. The '94 cab should be superb when it fully matures in six to eight years. Aged thirty months in sixty-gallon French oak barrels. Elegant balance, and firm tannic structures in perfect counterpoint to the richness of the oak. The '95 century vines zinfandel is quite good and moderately priced, if that is a consideration." His tone indicated he thought it might well be in my case. "The zin was *Gourmet* Magazine's pick-of-the-month not long ago. Supple, texturally distinctive, assertive."

"I'll try a bottle of the zinfandel."

"Certainly, sir."

He went and got me one. "Moderately priced" turned out to be twenty-four dollars; I managed not to wince. Kerry had a taste for better-quality wine, though not quite to the twenty-four-buck degree, and I wouldn't know a supple and texturally distinctive zinfandel from a jug of good Dago red no matter how aggressively it asserted itself. Well, you're never too old to learn to enjoy some of the finer things in life.

I gave my attention to the label. And the similiarity between its styling and that of the paintings by Janice Erskine was apparent even to my untrained eye. Narrowly ovoid in shape, outlined boldly in silver, it depicted a sparkling creek winding out of a dark line of trees, the trees black silhouettes with daubs of vivid green for contrast. Above the design was a silver crest incorporating gnarly old vines and clusters of grapes. Below, in descending rows: *Silver Creek Cellars • 1995 Century Vines Zinfandel • Woolfox Family Reserve • Alexander Valley • Estate Bottled.* Silver, black, and white. Sharply delineated lines and angles. No shading. The only real differences were in the spartan use of white and the added colors: the green in the trees and "Silver Creek Cellars" in a deep blue edged in silver and black. I squinted at it up close, to see if there was an artist's signature. There wasn't.

I asked the clerk, "Would you have any idea who designed the label?"

"I'm afraid not, sir. Is it important?"

"It might be very important."

"Then I suggest you contact Mr. Woolfox at the winery."

"He's the owner?"

"James Woolfox. The name is quite well known in the wine-making industry. Mr. Woolfox's father founded the Oak Barn label in the Sonoma Valley. Oak Barn remained in the family for several years after the elder Woolfox died, under his son's direction, before Mr. Woolfox divested to European interests." Meaning, I thought, the European interests had made him an offer he couldn't refuse. "Then he moved to the Alexander Valley and founded Silver Creek Cellars."

"Large or small operation?"

"Oh, quite small. I don't believe Silver Creek's annual production exceeds a thousand cases of any of its wines, and only a few hundred cases of each of its signature reds."

So arranging an audience with James Woolfox, or someone who could tell me what I wanted to know, ought not to be too difficult. It meant a drive up to the Alexander Valley—handling it by phone was too iffy—but I didn't mind that; my schedule for tomorrow was free. Tonight, though, I still had a couple of things to do before I could go home to Kerry, the first being a stop at the office to tell my opportunistic assistant that she would have to wait a while longer for a raise in her weekly salary.

The building on Valencia a few doors west of Eighteenth Street was an old, scabrous, two-story pseudo-Victorian with chipped plaster cornices and a once-white paint job that fog and rain and city dirt had turned a peppery gray. Wedged in tight against its neighbors, as were most of the buildings along here. The entire downstairs housed a busy tacqueria; upstairs, behind lightless and unmarked windows, there'd be two or more small offices or maybe a combination of office and living space.

I found a parking spot a few doors beyond and sat watching night settle on the litter-edged street. This was the Mission District, near the heart of it—one of the city's older and poorer neighborhoods, once populated mostly by Irish immigrants, now mostly by Latinos. If you had an adventurous turn of mind, or if you were young and carefree and fearless, you could find more or less healthy amusements in the Mission: swing-jazz nightclubs, hipster-trendy tapas clubs, sixties-style cafés that offer espresso and cappuccino and the latest hybrid in avant-garde poetry. But there is a much darker side to the neighborhood. Latino gangs have a strong hold there; drive-by and sidewalk shootings are not uncommon. Drug dealers flourish in the four-block radius around Sixteenth and Mission known to law enforcement as the Devil's Quadrangle, and muggers prowl both inside and outside the Quad. Unless you live or work there, it's not a good idea to leave your car unattended or to go wandering on the side streets after dark.

There was no mystery as to why Eberhardt had located his one-man agency here. The rents on Valencia are still fairly affordable, by city standards; and it's a short two-mile drive uphill from there to his house in Noe Valley. Still, the address had been a poor business decision. To anyone familiar with San Francisco, it branded his operation as small, undercapitalized, probably second-rate, and—unfairly—on the shady side. Corporate clients, unless they were like Barney Rivera and Great Western Insurance and had a working history with Eberhardt, would automatically have gone elsewhere. And he wouldn't have gotten many of the small-business and private-individual trade that are a necessary portion of an investigator's client list. Not after one good look at that building back there.

I sat for the better part of ten minutes, during which time a homeless panhandler got into a shouting match with a reluctant passerby, a drunk staggered into a dark doorway and sat or passed out with one leg jutting from the shadows as if severed, and what might have been a casual drug buy went down—all this, and it wasn't even seven o'clock. I itched to start the car, drive straight up to Diamond Heights and Kerry. But I'd talked myself out of coming last night, and I had no justification for backing out a second night. I'd promised Cliff Hoyt I would have this sifting among the bones of Eberhardt's life finished by the first of next week, and for my own sake as well as Bobbie Jean's I'd better be as good as my word.

I got out and locked the car, turned my collar up against the cold wind, and walked back to the building. The tacqueria was doing a brisk early-evening business; the aromas of cooked chiles and fried chorizo and tortillas crisping in lard stirred my gastric juices. Heart-attack country in there, but if I'd allowed myself I could have easily choked down a burrito, a couple of tacos, maybe a chile relleno. Instead I stepped into the darkened doorway next to the restaurant's entrance and used my pen flash to read the nameplates on the three mailboxes.

Eberhardt Investigative Services— #3. On the ring of keys Cliff Hoyt had given me was one for the mailbox; I used it and fished out a thin cluster of envelopes. Not much after more than a week's worth of deliveries: half a dozen pieces, at least the one on top junk mail. I put the envelopes into my pocket without looking through them, found the key that fit the entrance door, and let myself in.

Narrow stairwell and a fairly steep flight of unlighted stairs that creaked and groaned under my weight. On one side, wallpaper had begun to peel off in flaky strips like diseased skin. I could smell mildew and dry rot and the lingering odors generated by faulty sewer piping. Worse in here than I'd thought. Not only a bad business address but a firetrap and a probable deathtrap if and when the next 7.0 earthquake hit the city.

Upstairs, a hallway bisected the building's width, one large office or suite of offices that took up the entire front half—the sign on the door said in both English and Spanish that it was a family counseling service—and two small offices at the rear. The far one's door wore a placard with "Eberhardt Investigative Services" lettered on it. A different key opened the door. I stepped inside, groped the wall for a light switch.

Christ.

It was like walking into a prison cell. First impression, and one that stayed with me the entire time I was there. Twelve-by-fourteen box, bare wood floor, walls bare except for two small glass-framed hangings. The simulated oak desk and battered swivel chair he'd bought when we first became partners. But the rest of his old office furniture—two clumsy file cabinets made of particle board, typewriter and typewriter stand, an old-fashioned porcelain water cooler—was missing. In one corner stood a stubby, cheap-looking, two-drawer metal file case, and on a pair of pull-out desk boards on either side of the chair were a computer and a printer. That was all. The office was completely empty otherwise.

I open my own agency, I'm my own boss. Angry words flung at me not long before he ended the partnership. *Prove to you and everybody else my way's just as good as yours, maybe better.*

His way. This way.

For no particular reason I went and looked at the wall hangings first. One was his investigator's certificate, issued by the State Board of Licenses; the other was a twelve-by-fifteen photograph of him and a dozen other cops in uniform at some sort of SFPD function. The photo was so old and so badly framed that it had begun to yellow and buckle at the edges. It wasn't familiar to me and there was nothing on it to identify when or where it had been taken. I wondered where it had come from, but not why he'd hung it here. Reality and illusion were difficult to separate now, but one thing I did know for sure about Eberhardt: The only thing he'd ever wanted to be was a cop and the only period in his life he'd been truly happy was during his time on the force.

I turned to the file cabinet. The cooking odors from the tacqueria were almost as strong up here, wafting through the floor, but they no longer made me hungry; now there was a faint sick feeling in my belly. I took a couple of deep breaths, kept on breathing through my mouth as I poked through the two drawers. One held paper files: hard-copy printouts of reports and research data, copies of invoices, business correspondence, paid bills, bank statements, and cancelled checks. It was only about three-quarters full. The other drawer contained computer diskettes, each one labeled. I left both drawers open and moved to the desk.

Its scarred top held nothing more than a rack with three of the stubby briar pipes he'd favored, a humidor, and a combination telephone and answering machine, the inexpensive kind made by Radio Shack. The computer and printer were both Tandys, also of Radio Shack manufacture. The message light on the answering machine blinked steadily; I punched the rewind and then the play button. Four messages, none more recent than the Friday before his death—three from Barney Rivera, saying only his name and "Call me" on the first two, and "Come on, Eb, we need to talk" on the last; and the fourth from PG&E's billing department, reminding Mr. Eberhardt that he had not paid his March statement and that his electricity would be shut off if he didn't bring his account current by the tenth of May.

I opened the kneehole drawer. Envelopes, a thin stack of contract forms similar to the kind I used, pens and paper clips and a book of stamps, and a thin file folder marked CURRENT and containing a couple of pieces of stationery headed "O'Hanlon Bros., Distributors." Left-side drawers: unused diskettes, paper for the printer, a small carton of white plastic garbage bags. The bags puzzled me for a few seconds, until I realized there would be no janitorial service in a building like this and Eberhardt would have had to bus his own trash. Top right-side drawer: address book and appointment calendar. I took those out, set them on the desktop. Lower right-hand drawer—

A fifth of Four Roses, half empty, and two dirty glasses.

It was such a cliché—bottle of bourbon in the bottom drawer of the private eye's desk—that it might've been funny in different circumstances. Not here, not in these circumstances. So Eberhardt hadn't confined his boozing to home or neighborhood saloons; he'd been drinking on the job, too. But there was no surprise in the discovery. If I'd thought about it hard enough, I could've guessed it would be like this, just like this.

Nothing more for me here. Time to get the hell out, away from the crisping tortillas and frying chorizo, away from the miasma of decay that seemed to emanate like an invisible gas from the walls and floor and ceiling. I stuffed all the paper files and used diskettes into one of the garbage bags, added the address book and appointment calendar. I would go through the files later, with Kerry's help in screening the diskettes on her PC, and then I'd destroy everything to ensure confidentiality to Eberhardt's clients. The rest of the items in the office could go to Goodwill or the Salvation Army or one of the Mission's ethnic charities. Cliff Hoyt could take care of arranging that, or hire somebody to do it. Once I walked out of this cell, I would never come back.

But before I did that I stood in the doorway and took one last look at the place where Eberhardt had spent most of his days over the past four years. And I wondered if Barney Rivera or Bobbie Jean or anyone other than Eberhardt had set foot in here before tonight, or if he'd spent all those long days and maybe a few nights sitting here alone, drinking Four Roses and waiting for the phone to ring. And wondering that, I could feel his pain the way I'd felt Ira Erskine's on Monday. Feel it and understand a little more clearly why he'd decided dying was preferable to living.

* * *

“Now this is interesting,” Kerry said when I walked into the condo. “A full garbage bag in one hand and a jug of wine in the other. What’s the occasion?”

“No occasion. No connection either. I went to Eberhardt’s office; this one bag is what I came away with. I’ll sort through it tomorrow, the next day—not tonight.”

“And the wine?”

I explained about that.

She said, “It looks expensive.”

“Nope. Moderately priced.”

Kerry took a closer look, and I was glad I’d peeled off the price tag. “Estate-bottled zinfandel? It must’ve cost at least fifteen dollars.”

“Nothing’s too good for you, my sweet. I’ll have you know this was *Gourmet* magazine’s pick of the month not long ago. Supple, texturally distinctive, assertive. Firm tannic structures, too.”

She gave me one of her looks.

“Besides,” I said, “by drinking the entire bottle before dinner you can get a nice buzz on. You and me together.”

“Must’ve been bad at Eberhardt’s office.”

“Bad enough. Shall we open the wine and let it assert itself?”

“I’ll get the corkscrew,” she said.

6

THE ALEXANDER VALLEY IS A NEARLY two-hour drive northeast of San Francisco, some distance above its more famous neighbors, the Napa and Sonoma valleys. Twenty-four miles long, gradually broadening toward its southern end, it lies between the small towns of Cloverdale and Healdsburg. Highway 101 runs along its western perimeter; so does the Russian River, the valley's main irrigation source, for two-thirds of its length. The most fertile sections are below the hamlet of Geyserville, where the river veers eastward and meanders down the center of the valley. That part is flat, bordered by low, rolling hills whose slopes and clefts are clotted with oak and madrone; the topsoil is so thick and rich, the weather so vineyard-perfect the whole year round, that the cabernet and zinfandel grapes grown there are considered to be among the best in the state.

Until the past decade or so, the Alexander had only a couple of resident wineries. Most of the vineyards were owned by absentee landlords and after harvesting, the grapes were hauled off to wineries located elsewhere. That began to change in the eighties, when northern California underwent its wine-production boom. Dozens of new, small wineries whose emphasis was on quality rather than quantity opened for business, most in the Napa and Sonoma valleys; but Dry Creek Valley, the Russian River Valley, and the Alexander each got their share of the entrepreneurial newcomers as well. Nearly twenty wineries now operate in the Alexander Valley, the best of them producing what is known in the trade as signature reds that rival any made elsewhere, including the overly aggrandized Napa Valley. Even I had known that before my talk with the wine shop clerk, which is testimony to how far and wide the word has spread.

The Alexander is a little too far north and a little out of the way to attract the volume of visitors from San Francisco and the East Bay cities that Napa and Sonoma do. The resident wineries might not like this fact, but I was all for it; if I were going on a wine-tasting outing I'd want to do it at a leisurely pace, without having to fight traffic and crowds or pay tasting fees or be limited to two or three in the number of types available for tasting at a given winery. In any event, at noon on Thursday the traffic was light all along Alexander Valley Road to its intersection with Highway 128, another two-laner that follows the north-south course of the river. I turned south on 128. Not many cars along there, either. A pleasant, relaxed drive in the country, past vineyards and oak groves, an occasional winery and small cattle ranch.

Silver Creek Cellars was at the southern tip of the valley. A sign at its graded but unpaved entrance lane said that the tasting room was open from ten until four-thirty daily. The winery buildings weren't visible until you'd gone a hundred yards or so along the lane; then the trees that screened them opened up and I saw two stone structures set some distance apart, the larger one on slightly higher ground. Both were built back into notches cut in the hillside and shaded by live oaks; a section of the creek that had given the place its name ran through the trees to the south. The buildings figured to be no older than Silver Creek Cellars itself, but they were so artfully made that they not only blended into the landscape but looked as though they'd been there half a century or more.

There was only one car in the parking area. I put mine alongside it. Unlike the fogbound city, the day up here was sunny and dry and mostly windless; the air smelled of the oaks and of the rich scent of fermenting grapes. The building higher up was probably a storage warehouse; a guy on a forklift trundled a pallet-load of oak barrels out through a doorway in its side as I crossed to the smaller building.

Inside, the temperature was ten degrees cooler and the dank cellar aroma twice as rich. The tasting room was at the far end of an aisleway between rows of huge oak and stainless-steel vats. A heavyset, red-haired woman in a white smock and a lean man in overalls were bent alongside one of the metal vats—conducting some sort of test on the wine it contained, judging from an open kit full of vials and other apparatus. The woman said, "There's too much residual sugar, dammit," and the man answered, "I just don't see how that's possible, Gail," as I passed.

The tasting room was small, filled with stacked cases and racks of bottles on display, the counter L-shaped and taking up most of two walls. Absent were the T-shirts and crest-embossed wineglasses and other tourist items most wineries peddle along with their vintages these days. Limited space may have been the reason, but it might also mean that James Woolfox cared more about making and showcasing premium wines than he did about ringing up a few extra bucks. The bottle of '95 Century Vines Zinfandel last night had been pretty wonderful.

Only two people occupied the stone-walled room, a woman behind the counter and a male customer in the process of buying half a dozen bottles of Chardonnay. I pretended to browse among the racked wines, waiting for the transaction to be completed and the customer to leave. Most of the bottles wore the distinctive silver, black, and white label, but there were a few 1994 vintages that carried a different and inferior label. That told me the new one had been designed sometime in '95, for the '95 bottling.

The man left as I was reading the label description on a bottle of '94 Sauvignon Blanc, which some neo Bulwer-Lytton had rhapsodized as being "ripe, soft, plump, a passionate delight to the tongue." Wine people get downright orgasmic about their product at times, as if you ought to be making love to it instead of drinking it.

When I stepped up to the counter, the woman—a taffy blond about forty—greeted me with a bright smile and said, "Welcome to Silver Creek Cellars" as if she meant it. She gestured to a blackboard on which half a dozen whites and reds were listed. "Our current selections. Would you care to start with our Reisling?"

I explained that I wasn't there to taste and asked if James Woolfox was on the premises. No, he wasn't. "You're a day early," she said.

"Early?"

"He's still in Los Angeles. Due back tonight. Is it business or—?"

"Not exactly. As a matter of fact, you may be able to help me." I tapped one of the bottles in the service well. "I'm looking for some information about this label."

". . . Our merlot?"

"No, the label itself. Can you tell me who designed it?"

"Why, yes. Sondra Nelson. It's wonderful, isn't it?"

"That it is. Is Sondra Nelson a local artist?"

"She isn't an artist. Well, not professionally."

"That sounds as though you know her."

"I ought to. She works here." The woman smiled again and added, "But not for long. At least not full-time."

"Oh? Why is that?"

"She and Mr. Woolfox are getting married."

"Is that right? Good for them."

"In July. They've been engaged nearly a year."

"You seem pleased about it."

"Oh, I am. Sandy's a nice person, and Mr. Woolfox . . . do you know him at all?"

"I haven't had the pleasure."

"Well, he's quite a catch. In every way."

"How long has Ms. Nelson been employed here?" I asked.

"Let's see . . . she came about six months after we opened."

"About two and a half years, then."

"Closer to three, actually."

"Did she know Mr. Woolfox before that?"

"No. He hired her through a newspaper ad."

"What sort of work?"

"Back then? Same as my job—tasting-room hostess."

"What does she do now?"

"Mr. Woolfox calls her our woman-of-all-trades. You know, PR work, advertising, special-events planning."

"Is she here today?"

"No, she went to Los Angeles with Mr. Woolfox. Why are you so interested in Sandy?"

"I think she may be a woman I've been trying to locate."

"Locate? Why?"

"Has to do with her past life."

"Oh, God, you mean something bad—?"

"Nothing like that, no. It involves a child from a former marriage."

". . . I didn't know Sandy was married before. Or that she had a child."

"Not one to talk about her past?"

"Not much. Hardly at all."

I handed her the photos of Janice Erskine. "Is this Sondra Nelson?"

Pretty soon she said, "Well . . . Sandy has dark hair. Short and curly."

"Facial resemblance?"

"I suppose so. Yes. How old are these pictures?"

"Four or five years."

"Sandy's about thirty, so that seems right . . ."

"Try to imagine this woman with short, curly, dark hair. Or Ms. Nelson with long, ash-blond hair. The same person?"

It took her another fifteen seconds to decide, but when she did she sounded positive enough. "Yes. That's Sandy."

"And you say she and Mr. Woolfox are due back tonight?"

"That's right. Originally they were going to stay until next week, but Sandy has jury duty starting Monday."

"Will she be here at the winery tomorrow?"

"As far as I know she will. Are you coming back to see her?"

"Probably not."

"Should I tell her you were here?"

"Not necessary. Someone she knows will contact her."

"Are you sure it's nothing that will hurt her or Mr. Woolfox? They're so much in love . . ."

"It won't affect her relationship with him," I said, and hoped I was right. If Sondra Nelson was Janice Erskine, then it seemed she had in fact kicked her drug habit and built a clean new life for herself here. She deserved as much happiness as she could find after she faced the imminent loss of her son.

Outside again, I noticed that the workman on the forklift was still bringing oak barrels out of the warehouse. By the time I walked up there, he and the lift were back inside. I waited until he reappeared with another load and set it down alongside the others, then approached him.

"Excuse me. Talk to you for a minute?"

He was a fortyish, burly guy wearing Levi's and a white T-shirt with purple lettering across the front: "I Heard It Through the Grapevine." He looked me over, shrugged, and switched off the lift's engine.

"What can I do you for?"

"I've got a couple of photographs here. Mind taking a look at them and telling me if you recognize the woman?"

"Woman, huh? What kind of photos?"

"One portrait, one snapshot."

"So she's got her clothes on? Too bad." He laughed at his own wit. "Okay, let's see 'em."

I passed them over. He took a good look at one, a shorter look at the other. "Sure," he said, "that's Sandy. Sandy Nelson. Boss's fiancée." He pronounced it "fee-ahn-cee."

"You're sure?"

"Positive. Hair's different now, brown and curly, but that's Sandy." He favored me with a man-to-man grin. "I oughta know. I'm her best friend's main man."

So. She'd designed the label, all the dates seemed to check out, and now I had double corroboration on a photographic

ID. Good enough for me. I could go to my client with reasonable assurance that I'd earned my fee and leave the rest of it up to him.

On the way back along Highway 128 I called Tamara on the car phone and told her what I'd found out. She already had a bare-bones report on the Erskine investigation in her computer; she said she'd add the new information and have a printout ready by the time I got back. Then I rang up the St. Francis. Ira Erskine wasn't in his room, and a hotel page didn't turn him up; I left a message for him to contact me between four and five-thirty today or first thing in the morning.

At the crossroads I stopped at a deli store for a quick sandwich. What with that and midafternoon freeway traffic, it was three-forty before I walked into the office. And Erskine was there waiting for me. Had been waiting for fifteen minutes. He'd come straight over, he said, as soon as he got my message.

Tamara had already given him the printout. She'd tried to have him wait for me, she told me later, but he'd wheedled her into obliging him. When he saw me he hopped up from one of the clients' chairs and grabbed my hand in a quick, hard grip. The direct eyes were almost hot with excitement. The pain still burned there, but unless you'd seen it before, felt its intensity as I had on Monday, you might have taken it for a different emotion—something close to joy.

"You're amazing," he said. "Three days. I was sure it would take longer . . . a week, two weeks."

"Well, we got lucky."

"The wine label, yes. Of all things. I never dreamed she'd make a mistake like that."

"Mistake?"

"Commercial art, I mean. She was so serious about her painting."

"She probably designed the label as a favor to Woolfox."

"Who? Oh, the winery owner. My God, a winery, of all places. We seldom drank wine, neither of us had a taste for it. But that was the whole idea, of course."

"What was?"

"Her new life. A completely new existence."

I sat down at my desk. Erskine remained standing, clutching the report the way a man might hang on to a lifeline. I hadn't expected him to take the news with this much feeling; he'd been under such tight control during Monday's interview. He was practically quivering.

"The important thing," I said, "is that she seems to be off drugs. Straight again."

"You didn't see her, did you?"

"No. Doesn't the report say she's returning tonight from a trip to L.A.?"

"Oh, that's right." He dragged a pack of Marlboros out of his shirt pocket, saw the look on my face, and put it away again. A nicotine hit was the last thing he needed right now. "I'm just wondering how she looks. Did anyone you talked to say how she looks?"

"Only that her hair is brown now, short and curly."

"Brown. Curly. She had such beautiful blond hair. So soft . . . Jesus, it was like satin . . ."

Almost sexual, the way he said that, as if bed memories were dancing in his head. He was beginning to embarrass and bother me a little. I asked him, "Did Ms. Corbin put in the report that Sondra Nelson and James Woolfox are being married in July?"

"Married?" His smile straightened into a flat line. "No, that's not in here."

"They've been engaged nearly a year. The person I talked to says she's very happy."

"It doesn't matter," Erskine said.

"Doesn't matter to you that she's happy?"

"No, the engagement. I don't care about that."

"Look, Mr. Erskine, I realize you still care for your ex-wife. But if you have some idea you can talk her into a reconciliation after all this time, I think you're letting yourself in for a serious disappointment."

He said "That's my business" with an edge to the words.

"And your son's." Edge in my voice, too. "That's the primary issue here, isn't it? The only reconciliation that really matters right now?"

He stared at me for a count of five; then the fire in him seemed to bank a little and he sat down abruptly. "I'm sorry," he said. "You're right. Absolutely right. I shouldn't let myself get so worked up. Tommy . . . of course Tommy's the primary issue. But I love Janice, now as much as I ever did, and the prospect of seeing her again . . . oh Christ, sometimes I feel as though I'm on a roller coaster and I can't get off. Have you ever felt that way?"

"More than once. But either you manage to stop the ride and get off under your own power, or it'll end up going so fast it'll throw you off."

He nodded. "I know. I'll be all right. I just need to see her again, talk to her about the boy, and then I'll be fine."

"Sure about that?"

"Yes. I'm sure."

"I'd hate to think you'd try to interfere in Sondra Nelson's wedding plans. Sondra Nelson now, not Janice Erskine or Janice Durian. Clean and happy in her new life."

"I won't interfere," he said. "I'll leave for Santa Fe after

I see her. Whether she comes along to be with Tommy or not is up to her."

"That's the right attitude."

He nodded again, folded the report in careful thirds and tucked it into his coat pocket, and took out his folder of traveler's checks. "How much do I owe you?"

"If you're running short we can send an invoice . . ."

"No, finances aren't a problem. I'd prefer to settle now."

I gave Tamara today's handful of expenses; she entered them and prepared and printed out a final bill. Erskine signed over another batch of checks, thanked Tamara, thanked me and shook my hand again, and was gone.

"Tell you something," Tamara said, "I'm not sorry to see the back end of that dude for good."

"That makes two of us."

"You got the strange hit off him, too, huh? This time?"

I shrugged. "Too much weighing on him," I said. "His emotions are all out of whack."

"Yeah. But no matter what he said, he cares more about seeing his ex again than about his kid dying and he's not gonna just talk to her once and leave her alone. Man's carrying a torch big as a house."

I didn't answer, but I was thinking the same thing. And wishing now, too late and despite their son's terminal illness, that I hadn't found Sondra Nelson and sent Erskine on his way to the Alexander Valley.

7

I SPENT THE EVENING ALONE IN MY flat, going through Eberhardt's paper files. It was cheerless work, as much for what they told me about his deteriorating mental state as for the cold, bleak facts they contained. When I was done I had a pretty good idea of the shape and substance of his professional life over the past four years, and of how it had contributed to his suicide. But with the exception of a couple of small question marks that may or may not have had any significance, I could find nothing past or present that pointed to the trigger.

He'd never been a very conscientious report-maker or record-keeper; during our partnership days, all his paperwork—client reports, expense accountings, research data—tended to be sloppily organized and incomplete. But in the first year or so of Eberhardt Investigative Services he'd made an obvious effort to be more painstaking. You could see a kind of stolid enthusiasm in his early transcripts and correspondence, his detailed financial records. I'd speculated once that opening his own agency was his way of taking charge of what remained of his life, recapturing both his dignity and a self-worth that had been badly eroded by a combination of factors, among them a dependance on me and an inability to forgive himself for the one huge mistake that had ended his police career. Those first-year documents intimated that I'd pretty much been right. He'd tried the best way he knew how to make a success of his new venture. Taken a strictly professional approach in everything he did, to the point of buying and learning to use a computer.

And still he'd failed. Not immediately, but inevitably. The fault wasn't his; the fault was competition, the stack of problems faced by every small businessman just starting out, the tenor of the times. There'd been a small flurry of activity in the beginning—friends and associates like Barney Rivera tossing bones to help him out. He'd done the work capably enough, but even when you build a string of repeat clients, as I had over a quarter of a century as an independent contractor, jobs are often sporadic. The big agencies, the ones with manpower and financial backing and technological know-how, get the cream; the rest of us have to scramble for the leavings. Eberhardt couldn't compete. I'd gotten work that might have gone to him, even though he knew the clients as well as I did, because of my experience and success rate; the same was true of other established contractors. He'd got through the first year and a half all right, mostly on handouts, low-end divorce work, and one profitable three-week stint as an investigator for the defense in a felony trial. Even so, there were two stretches of more than two weeks each when he hadn't worked at all, and his total gross income for the first five and a half months was only $13,800, the first full year just $23,000 and change.

His second full year he'd had a quarter fewer jobs and

made six thousand less than the first. The third year: $9,987.00. And for the first four months of this year: $1,150.00

The quality and quantity of his record-keeping reflected the downward spiral. The stolid enthusiasm disappeared after fifteen months or so; the reports grew thinner, less detailed, and if it was plain enough to me that he'd begun expending less effort on the skip-traces and insurance claims and divorce work, it had to've been just as plain to the clients. The professionalism had crumbled in other ways, too. By the beginning of last year he was cutting corners. There were indications that he overbilled on the number of hours it took him to finish a job. And I was pretty sure in two cases, both new corporate clients, that he'd done some expense-account padding—and none too creatively, since neither of the clients brought him repeat business.

This year, from January first to the last week in April, he'd had just three jobs: a personal background check, a Great Western claims investigation that he'd done a poor job on, and the liquor distributor's theft stakeout. The first two had taken him eight days total, and he'd spent five days and nights on the O'Hanlon Brothers job. Thirteen days of work in four months. And the rest of the time? Drinking, brooding, building his own private gallows day by day, board by board. No clients, no prospects, no money. He'd never been much of a saver; as far as I knew, he'd had no more than a few thousand in the bank when he busted up our relationship. Most of that would've been spent in setting up his agency and the rest would've disappeared by the second year. The bank statements on his business account showed a balance at the end of last month of $36.18; they also showed periodic charges for overdrawn checks, nearly a dozen of them, and over the past eighteen months more than a dozen small deposits of between $100 and $300. So he and Bobbie Jean had been living on her salary at least that long and probably longer, and she'd also been feeding him enough cash so he could keep his office rent and utilities and other expenses more or less current. And her job at a San Rafael real estate brokerage company couldn't have brought in much more than $35,000 a year gross. The Elizabeth Street house was paid for, but city property taxes are high and so are utilities; they must've been just squeaking by. More blows to Eberhardt's pride. Another few boards for the gallows.

I took a close look at the three jobs he'd had this year. An item in the CURRENT file flagged my attention: one of the sheets of stationery headed "*O'Hanlon Bros., Distributors*" contained a list of eleven names and addresses. Employees or former employees of the firm? Possible suspects in the liquor thefts? A single name on the list had been heavily circled in felt-tip pen: Danny Forbes, with an address on Silliman Street in the Portola district. The circled name interested me enough to pull the sheet and set it aside.

Eberhardt's appointment calendar had no notations for the week before his death and only one for last week. That one was for the day prior, his last full day on this earth: *Disney, 2:00, Tues.* The name was unfamiliar and I couldn't find it in his address book.

The book had about twenty-five entries, a couple of which were scratched out—one, a bail bondsman I'd worked for a few times, with such apparent anger that the pen he'd used had ripped through the paper. Only five of the names were unknown to me, all of which appeared to be businesses of one kind and another. But he hadn't dealt with any of them recently, judging from his phone bills and copies of his correspondence.

The most recent phone bills were among the handful of envelopes I'd lifted from the mailbox. No long-distance or toll calls from his office number; whatever calls he'd made from there had been local and Pac Bell doesn't list those on its statements. The other bill was from Cellular One, which does list all outgoing cell phone calls. Why Eberhardt had continued to pay high mobile-phone rates, when he and Bobbie Jean were living hand to mouth, escaped me—unless a cell phone had been some sort of symbol to him, an independence lifeline that hadn't done him a bit of good. He'd given up his life before he'd given up his portable phone. In any event, that bill listed a total of six outgoing calls over the ten days prior to his death: the first and last to his home number, the one to my office, one to Barney Rivera at Great Western, one that I matched to O'Hanlon Brothers, and one that I was unable to match to any in his address book or elsewhere. That one had been made at 1:07 last Tuesday afternoon, and had lasted a minute or less. A connection to the two o'clock appointment with Disney, whoever Disney was? I wrote the name and number down in my notebook.

Finished, I sat looking at all the papers piled on my desk and on the living-room floor. Nearly four years of a man's professional life, and every damn bit of it would go into the trash. Not a single scrap of paper worth saving. And all I knew now that I hadn't known when I started was that Eberhardt's four-year descent had been a little worse than I'd originally believed. He hadn't just been a despondent drunk; he'd turned into a careless and pettily deceitful drunk. If he'd set out to recapture his dignity and self-worth, he'd wound up trampling on what was left of both.

Sad, pathetic. And one more piece of proof that the real Eberhardt had been hidden from me all along, that the one

I'd called my friend for thirty-some years had been shadow and silhouette, sham and mirage.

From the office Friday morning I called the number I'd copied into my notebook. A recorded voice came on after three rings. "You have reached the offices of Richard H. Disney, Ph.D. If you would like to make an appointment, or if you have other business, please leave your name and number at the tone. Office hours are Monday through Thursday, nine-thirty to four-thirty . . ."

I hung up without waiting for the rest. The Ph.D. after the man's name could mean a few different things, but the one I thought of first was head doctor. I dragged out and consulted the city's yellow pages. And under Psychologists I found Richard H. Disney, Ph.D., with an address on Church Street.

So Eberhardt had been seeing a shrink. The combination of booze and depression must have driven him to it. And yet unburdening himself to another person, and a psychologist at that, didn't seem to be something he would've done; he'd always expressed distrust of and contempt for "brain pickers." That was one facet of the man I felt pretty sure I was right about. No way could I picture him in a psychologist's office, admitting he was a drunk and a failure and that he'd lost his will to live.

Bolt Street was a hive of activity early on a Friday afternoon. Semis, trailers, pickups, forklifts, workmen, engine noise, and a miasma of diesel clogged its dead-end half block so thoroughly that I didn't even try to penetrate it. I turned onto the cross street and found parking there instead. And at that, walking the alley was more hazardous than driving it: a reckless jitney driver nearly mowed me down before I reached the O'Hanlon Brothers' loading dock.

Two of the three bays were occupied, and half a dozen men wheeled hand trucks back and forth between the open maw of the warehouse and the yawning backsides of two big trailers. I asked one of the men where I might find T. K. O'Hanlon; according to Eberhardt's CURRENT file, that was the brother who'd hired him. "In his office, probably," the guy said, and pointed out a tunnellike walkway that led through the warehouse to an office area at the rear. I did some more talking there and was eventually granted an audience with T. K. O'Hanlon in his private sanctum. Which turned out not to be very private: one entire wall was made of glass and looked out into the cavernous warehouse with its crates and cartons and pallets and bins and shelves of enough varieties of booze to make Andrew Volstead and Elliot Ness revolve in their graves.

O'Hanlon cut an impressive figure, in the sense that a large and crudely crafted outdoor sculpture is impressive. He looked as though he'd been assembled out of a bunch of different-size square blocks tightly fitted together: square head on top of square shoulders on top of a square torso. Even his hips seemed square, his legs and arms squarish elongations. The face block had gouges for eyes, a crooked slash for a mouth, and a knob for a nose, and was surmounted by a colorless bristle like dried-up moss on a rock. The eyes were quick and shrewd, though. Anyone who formed an opinion about T. K. O'Hanlon based solely on his appearance would be making a serious error in judgment.

He sized me up, too, as we shook hands, and evidently I passed muster. His tone was cordial enough when he said, "Friend of Eberhardt's, eh? Hell of a thing, him bumping himself off out there on the street. We had cops in here asking questions and getting in the way most of the morning after it happened."

I had no comment to make on that.

He said, "So what brings you here now? I'm not in the market for any more private cops, if that's it. Not yet anyhow."

"That's not it, Mr. O'Hanlon. I—"

"T. K.," he said. "Everybody calls me T. K."

"All right, T. K. I'm not looking for business, I'm looking for answers. To why he killed himself."

"Little late for that, isn't it?"

"Not as far as I'm concerned."

O'Hanlon shrugged. "You were his friend and you don't have any idea, how should I? Drunks do crazy things. I should've known better than to hire a drunk. Like hiring a fat woman to catch a thief in a candy factory."

"If you knew he had a drinking problem going in, why did you hire him?"

"He worked cheap, that's why. My brother and I can't afford to pay what some of you guys charge. I called around, I got some estimates, he gave me the one we could afford. You get what you pay for, like they say."

I let that pass, too.

"No offense," O'Hanlon said. "He's dead, it's a hell of a thing, but facts are facts. One thing T. K. O'Hanlon doesn't trade in and that's bullshit. My wife says I got as much tact as a rolling pin."

"About the job you hired Eberhardt to do, T. K."

"Find out which one of our employees been ripping us off, yeah. More than a hundred cases the past few months—single-malt Scotch, sour-mash bourbon, Napoleon brandy. Ten, eleven thousand bucks' worth, and the insurance don't even begin to make up for it."

"Was he getting anywhere?"

"Nope. I ask what he's finding out, he tells me he's working on it, these things take time. Far as I could tell, he mostly just sat out there on the street nights hoping for something to fall into his lap. And he wasn't there all the time he said he was."

"How do you know he wasn't?"

"I came in last Saturday night about eleven, doing a favor for a friend. He wasn't on the street then. Chances are he wasn't there part of Sunday night, either."

"No?"

"Nick and me got ripped off again that weekend. Nick's my kid brother. Played pro ball with the Detroit Lions in the seventies, maybe you remember him? Three years, linebacker and special teams before he screwed up his knee."

"I remember him," I lied. "How much was stolen that time?"

"Five cases of Glenlivet and two of sour mash, part of a special order for a customer. Shipment came in on Saturday morning—we work half days on Saturdays—and the inventory was short on Monday."

"What did Eberhardt say when you told him about it?"

"Admitted he was gone part of Saturday night. Hour or so, he said, to get something to eat. Buy more booze for himself is more like it. Said he was here all of Sunday night. You know what I think? If he was here Saturday and Sunday, he was passed out in his car both nights. Whole squadron of thieves could've emptied the warehouse, carried everything out right past him and he wouldn't've noticed."

His bluntness nettled me, even though he was probably

right. I held down a sharp retort, handed him the sheet of company stationery containing the list of names and addresses. "Did you give this to Eberhardt? I found it in his files."

"Yeah. He asked for it first thing, people I had any reason to suspect. Former employees, most of 'em."

"Who circled that one name? You or him?"

"Wasn't me. Forbes, eh? I wouldn't be surprised."

"If Danny Forbes is the thief? Why do you say that?"

"We got twenty people working for us, a dozen in the warehouse. I'd lay odds seventeen, eighteen are either stone honest or too timid to steal from us. I figure maybe three guys still on the payroll have the balls to do it. Forbes is one."

"Why him specifically?"

"Why?" O'Hanlon thought about it. "He's got an attitude, that's one reason. Little guy, good worker but always acting tough, like it'll make him bigger than he is. Got in a fight with a teamster on the loading dock once, man almost twice his size—nearly had his head torn off. Got the crap beat out of him the weekend those last seven cases disappeared, too."

"Oh? Here, you mean?"

"In some bar near where he lives. Showed up on Monday morning with his nose bent out of shape and a cut over one eye. Guy shoved him, he shoved back, boom! he's on his ass and breathing sawdust. That kind never learns."

"Does he have a key to this place?"

"Key? Him? Hell, no. Nick and me are the only ones have keys. New locks. I had 'em changed when the thefts started, not that I expected it'd do much good."

"Why not?"

"Too easy to get in and out, if you been working here long

enough. Old doors, old windows, and too many for tight security. Guy like Forbes could figure ways in and out without too much trouble. Only real way for us to safeguard the inventory is to have all new doors and windows or an alarm system installed, and either one'd cost us five times as much as we been losing on the stolen liquor."

"Why don't you just fire Forbes and the other two?"

"You think I wouldn't like to? I'd kick 'em out in a New York minute if it wasn't for their union. Nick and me, we treat our people right and we have good relations with all the unions, can't afford to get 'em down on our necks, but sometimes the rules are a pain in the hinder . . . Ah, hell, why bitch about something you can't do anything about?"

"You single out Forbes when you first talked to Eberhardt?"

"Not exactly. Just told him what I told you—Forbes and Barnes and King are the three still working for us that're capable of it."

But Eberhardt hadn't circled Barnes or King; he'd circled Forbes. Why? If he'd found out anything incriminating against the man, there was no indication of it in his file . . .

O'Hanlon had turned to the glass wall and was surveying his domain. Pretty soon he motioned to me, and when I joined him he said, "See that guy over there by the liqueur bins? On your right there. That's Forbes."

Danny Forbes was a little guy, all right—thin, sinewy, with a mop of red hair and the kind of face that would contract into a belligerent glare three times as often as it would open up into a smile. He was stacking cases in a row of floor bins, working at a steady pace.

"If he is the one," O'Hanlon said, "I'll be the next man to knock him on his skinny ass. And it won't be long, either. Another big shipment's coming in next week and Nick and me got plans to stake out the place ourselves. Catch the son-of-a-bitch red-handed."

"Suppose he lays off this one?"

"He better not. We haven't got time to stake out every new shipment comes in. Bastard does lay off, maybe I'll be in the market for another private eye after all. How much you charge by the day?"

"More than you'd be willing to pay. Not interested, T. K."

"Too bad. I like you, the way you handle yourself—real professional. Too bad I didn't pick you out of the phone book instead of that lush Eberhardt. We'd've got along fine, you and me."

I doubted it. But I managed to get out of there without telling him so and lowering his already less-than-exalted opinion of private detectives.

On the way back downtown I detoured by the Hall of Justice to see Jack Logan. Jack is a lieutenant in General Works, Eberhardt's old rank and detail. The two of them had worked together for a lot of years, been good friends before Eberhardt took his early retirement. But their friendship, too, had faded with the years. After the end of the regular poker game that had included the three of us, Joe DeFalco, and Barney Rivera, they'd seen little of each other. Jack hadn't had any contact with him at all, he'd told me, in ten months.

He was in but busy, so I had to wait fifteen minutes before he called me into his office. He said he couldn't give me much time; I said I didn't need much, and told him briefly why I was there. A few more creases appeared in his lined face; he lifted a hand to rumple his already rumpled gray hair.

He said, "What makes you think this Danny Forbes might be involved in Eb's death?"

"I don't think that. I'm just poking around, trying to make sense of what happened. You know me, Jack."

"Oh, yeah, I know you." He punched up the file on his computer, studied the screen. "Nothing there at all. Forbes is a bowler, bowls Tuesday nights in a mixed doubles league in Daly City. He was in bed with one of the women in the league, her apartment in D.C., when Eb died."

"That kind of alibi is never too solid."

"In this case, it is."

"Does Forbes have a record?"

He checked the file. "No felony arrests."

"What about the alleged bar fight he got into two weekends ago?"

"What about it? Happened days before Eb shot himself." Jack leaned back in his chair, folded his hands across his paunch. He's nearing retirement and tends now and then to adopt an avuncular pose, even with someone his own age. "You can't make a murder case out of this."

"I'm not trying to."

"Aren't you? It was suicide and no mistake. Everything says so: his drinking, his mental state, the circumstances, the note in the glove box, the fact that it was his gun and only his prints were on it—"

"Three-fifty-seven Magnum," I said. "That's a big piece. Take some effort to angle it against your own chest. And why do it that way? Why not in the mouth, or against the temple?"

"For Chrissake, man, who knows what goes through a suicide's mind in those last seconds? Maybe he couldn't bring himself to eat the bullet. Maybe he was too drunk to be thinking much at all. A chest shot takes some maneuvering but it's not uncommon. Powder burns on his shirt, nitrate traces on his hand—*he* fired the round."

"All right."

"Suicide. Period. The investigating inspectors know it and I know it and you know it, too. Nobody likes it when a cop, a friend, blows himself away, but it happens and it happened in this case. Why don't you give yourself a break and accept it, put it behind you like the rest of us are trying to do?"

"Yeah," I said, as much to myself as to Logan. "Why the hell don't I?"

8

Elizabeth Street, climbing one of the hillsides in the upper reaches of Noe Valley, is old residential San Francisco—quiet, middle-class, single-family houses on good-size lots and the neighborhood not much changed since Eberhardt and Dana bought their house shortly after they were married forty years ago. It was a large two-story frame with an open front yard and an attached garage—the one joint possession he'd insisted on keeping as part of the divorce settlement. Until four years ago he'd maintained the property well enough, but he seemed not to have bothered much since. Its green-and-brown paint job was flaked and peeling, one of the porch railings had been broken and left unrepaired, weeds and untrimmed shrubbery made a jungly nest of the yard.

"My God," Kerry said when we drove up in front late Saturday morning, and I said, "Yeah, but I'm not surprised." Neither of us had been by here since the estrangement.

Kerry hadn't wanted to come with me. It had taken part of the morning to wear down her resistance, convince her that misery needs if not loves company. After all, I'd reminded her, she was the one who'd caved in first to Bobbie Jean and committed herself to the task of sifting and sorting right along with me. I may not know my wife as well as she knows me, but if I work at it I can usually push the right buttons and get her to agree to just about anything within reason.

We'd brought cardboard cartons with us; I hauled four out of the trunk and up onto the porch. The mailbox was stuffed full, and a number of magazines, catalogues, and oversize pieces of junk mail were strewn on the floor underneath. Bills, more junk, a letter to Bobbie Jean from somebody in South Carolina. I put all of it into one of the cartons while Kerry unlocked the door.

The place looked better inside, more or less the way I remembered it. Bobbie Jean's domain and she'd always been a tidy housekeeper. Shadows filled the living room, but I could make out the shapes of the old familiar furniture, the big fireplace, the wall hangings. But what I stood staring at was the section of carpet stretching from the hallway into the living room. Less than ten years old, this carpet. The original, the one I was seeing in my mind's eye, had been replaced on account of the bloodstains—blotches and smears that had soaked into the wool nap and couldn't be eradicated. Little prickles of cold moved along my back. So much blood . . .

Sunday afternoon in August, nine years ago, not long after Dana left him for her Stanford professor. Eberhardt and me in the backyard drinking beer, commiserating while we wait for the coals in the barbecue to whiten. We step inside to open two more cans, ready the steaks, and the doorbell rings and he goes to answer it. I hear his voice exclaim, "What the hell—" and then the two gunshots, and I run in there and he's down and the shooter is framed in the doorway with the smoking gun in his hand; and before I can react he pops me once, high in the chest, and I'm down, too, and he's gone and I crawl around in my own blood until I reach Eberhardt, see the hole in his belly and the wound on the side of his head, and I think he's dead, I think I must be dying, too . . .

The memory was so painfully sharp it might have happened a week or two ago instead of nine long years. The shooter, a hired gun, had been after Eberhardt and I'd gotten caught in the wrong place at the wrong time. And all because the honest, crook-hating cop had slipped and taken a bribe. And when he'd tried to back out, the man who had corrupted him had made him a target. The bribe nearly cost both of us our lives. It had cost Eberhardt his career. Not because the department found out about it, but because I did; and when I confronted him he'd seemed unable to forgive himself for what he'd done. If he had opted to sweep the whole thing under the rug I might have let him get away with it, but it would have ended our friendship and he didn't want that on his conscience, too, he said. But he also hadn't wanted to lose his pension, so he'd compromised by taking the early retirement. The easy way out for both of us. A man shouldn't have to be punished for the rest of his life for one mistake, should he? An honest man, a good cop, a friend?

I never took anything in thirty years—not a nickel, not even a cup of coffee. His words to me in the hospital, after the shooter and the one who'd hired him had gotten what was coming to them. *Tempted a couple of times; who doesn't get tempted? But I never gave in. I didn't think it was in me to give in . . . But things happen. Some things you prepare for, like you get old and tired. Some things you don't prepare for, because you figure they can't happen.*

Like your wife walking out on you, taking up with some other guy. Taking the guts right out of your life. You say to yourself: I got to hang on, it'll all work out. So you hang on. What the hell else can you do? But then maybe you get tempted again, one day right out of the blue. Not small potatoes this time, a whole goddamn feast. And all you got to do is look the other way on something nobody gives a damn about anyway. You get mad, you say no at first—but maybe you keep on listening. And maybe you break open inside and for a little while you stop caring. And maybe the no turns to yes.

I'd thought I understood, and so I'd been the one to forgive, but now I wasn't so sure. Could be he'd stopped caring for good back then. And some or all of what he'd said to me had been lies or bullshit. Could be he'd been jerking me around, playing me so I'd do just what I did—let him off the hook, take him in as a partner, teach him the ropes and carry him until he didn't need me anymore. One thing for sure: I couldn't forgive him again, for what he'd done to himself and to Bobbie Jean—

"Hey, are you okay?" Kerry's voice in my ear, and a nudge to go with it. She'd turned on the lights; the shadows were gone. Her face, close to mine, showed concern.

"Yeah. Little trip down memory lane, that's all."

"Bad trip, from your expression. The time you and Eb were shot?"

I nodded. "Faster we get done and out of here, the better I'll like it."

"Where do you want to start?"

"Upstairs. I'll take his study, you do the bedroom."

We climbed the creaky staircase, went separate ways at the top. The last door on the left had originally led to a third bedroom; he'd converted it into a study for himself. More shadows, and the faint, stale residue of the lousy pipe tobacco he'd smoked. I opened the curtains partway to let it daylight. Everything in there was as I remembered it, too. Desk, sideboard, Naugahyde couch, overstuffed chair, bookcase with some out-of-date police manuals and a few other books stuffed into it, an electric Olympia beer sign on one wall. The framed photograph of our Police Academy graduating class was missing; so was his model train layout. Took the photo down because I was in it, maybe. Got rid of the model train because he'd lost interest in it, just as he'd lost interest in everything else that had once mattered to him.

At first it seemed that he hadn't spent much time in here recently. The desktop was bare except for a telephone and a rack of pipes, and thin layers of dust had settled throughout. But then I saw that the ashtray on the chair arm was full of dottle, that a dirty glass and a nearly empty fifth of Four Roses were on the sideboard. And over near the chair you could still smell the bourbon that had slopped onto the carpet. He'd spent time in here, all right, the same as always. Sitting and smoking and swilling cheap whiskey. He'd called this room his sanctuary; Dana hadn't been allowed in and Bobbie Jean probably hadn't been, either. In the last year or so the sanctuary had turned into a drunkard's crib.

I knelt in front of the sideboard. His safe was built into the bottom, concealed by a sliding panel. Small, just large enough to hold documents and a few valuables. I removed a full bottle of Four Roses and some extra glasses, slid the panel aside to expose the dial. He'd given me the combination long ago, "in case of emergency," and I'd written it down in an old address book that I'd dug out last night. I wouldn't have been surprised if he had changed the combination, but it was still the same. So were some of the contents I'd seen the one other time I'd opened it. A small jewelry case that contained his wedding ring; his marriage license and final divorce decree; two insurance policies, both lapsed. None of it seemed to have been touched in a long time. Nine years ago the safe had also held his bribe—one thousand shares of stock in an electronics outfit that could have eventually been worth as much as six figures if the company had prospered—and fifteen hundred dollars in U.S. savings bonds, a bank savings passbook, and an envelope with a small amount of cash. All that was gone now. Long gone.

The desk next. In addition to a welter of canceled checks, paid bills, and other household records, all more than sixteen months old, I found his checkbook and current check register. The register contained two puzzling entries. On the Tuesday before his death he had made a deposit of five hundred dollars to his account; and he had also written a check in the exact same amount to an unspecified payee, just the date and amount noted. The deposit receipt was tucked in there and it told me the five hundred had all been in cash. Where had he had gotten that much in one lump? And who had been the recipient?

I put the checkbook and register in my pocket, then emptied the drawer into one of the cardboard cartons and added the contents of the safe. Bobbie Jean wouldn't want any of it, but I saw no reason to leave it for the Hoyts to deal with.

Carrying the box, I went down to the master bedroom. Kerry was coming out of the walk-in closet with a plastic-draped sport coat on a hanger. A few other articles of clothing were laid out on the bed. When she saw me she said, "This coat and those things there are brand-new, never worn. Presents, I suppose. Bobbie Jean can have them sold in a consignment shop if she needs the money. Otherwise . . . Well, I thought I'd separate them out anyway."

"Anything else?"

"His jewelry case. Cufflinks, tie tacks, a gold chain, half a dozen silver dollars, and some other old coins."

"That all?"

"In the case? Yes."

"You know what I mean."

"I'd've told you if there was."

I left her to finish up in there and wandered downstairs. In the living room was another desk, the small kind with a hinged flap that folds up when you're not using it. The more current household records were in there, all the checks written in Bobbie Jean's spidery hand. Eberhardt had always done his own bill-paying; the fact that Bobbie Jean had taken over sixteen months ago meant that he'd either lost interest or fouled up the accounts as a result of his drinking. Without going through any of the papers, I dumped them all in with the stuff from upstairs and then set the box in the hallway.

There was nothing else worth bothering with in the living room. I went into the kitchen. More unpleasant memories: My last visit four years ago, after Eberhardt called off his planned marriage to Bobbie Jean. He'd been hung over that day, his eyes looking as though he were bleeding internally; out boozing the night before, wallowing in self-pity. I'd flung angry words at him about that and about driving drunk, and they'd escalated into an attack on his careless work habits. *I've spent half my time either doing your work or covering your ass . . . When are you going to grow up, accept responsibility?* We were here in the kitchen then, him sucking down orange juice for his hangover thirst. And he'd flung angry words back at me. *You come into my house and dump shit all over me, now it's my turn. Hard to get along with . . . reckless as hell . . . self-righteous pain in the ass . . .* Standing nose-to-nose, trading insults, and I'd lost my temper and shoved him, and he'd bull-rushed me, and my unthinking reaction was to hit him. Sucker-punch in the gut, not pulling it, putting him on the floor and then afterward into the bathroom to vomit. Kid stuff; I'd regretted it instantly, tried in vain to smooth it over. Hurt pride, fuel for the grudge he'd never stopped nursing. But our friendship and our partnership had been dead for him long before that. If it hadn't been for that stupid punch in the belly, he'd have found some other excuse to walk.

Same thing last Wednesday morning, I thought. Ready to go out, and all he'd needed was a final excuse.

I didn't linger in the kitchen, the hell with it. I shoved through the connecting door into the garage. Years ago he'd turned it into a home workshop, cramming it so full of woodworking equipment he'd had to park his car and Bobbie Jean hers in the driveway or on the street. Another of his lost interests: dust everywhere, rust on the blade teeth on his table saw and band saw, a half-finished table so long abandoned the wood showed cracks and mildew stains under its dust shroud. Maybe Joe DeFalco could use some of this stuff; he collected and restored antique gambling equipment, his one passion other than newspaper work, and he had a workshop of his own. I made a mental note to ask him next time we talked.

Against the rear wall was a storage area. Most of what was there was junk, but among the litter was the metal locker in which he'd kept his fishing gear. It was all still there gathering dust and cobwebs: spinning rods and fly rods, including the Dennis Bailey parabolic bamboo rod that had been his favorite; reels and hip boots and the beat-up rattan creel he'd had since he was a kid; tackle box and the two big fly cases. I opened one fly case, then the other. Nymphs, streamers, dry flies, wet flies. Bugs with names like Bitch Creek Special and Gray Fox Variant. Dozens of top-quality lures, among them two I'd always admired—a #8 Jay-Dave Hopper and a #12 Hairwing Coachman for better visibility in heavy water. I hesitated, looking at the flies. Take them along? At least the Hopper and the Coachman . . . maybe the Bailey fly rod, too? It would be a shame to let them go to Goodwill and some fisherman who might not appreciate them. But did I want even this much of a reminder of him, the fishing trips we'd taken together to Black Point and the Sierras, the good times before the bad?

No, I thought, no. I don't want anything of his. Not a goddamn thing.

I shut the locker, went back inside the kitchen. Kerry had come down and was halfheartedly poking around in there. She shook her head; I shook mine. Her expression said she was already fed up with this morbid bone-picking and couldn't we for God's sake hurry it up and go home?

We hurried. Another forty-five minutes and we were through with the rest of the rooms and all the closets. And what we had separated out, including the articles of clothing from the bedroom, fit into just three cartons. So damn little worth saving, and at that, some if not most of what we were carrying away—the household records, for one thing—would eventually be discarded or given away to strangers.

A man lives sixty years and this is all he leaves behind in the way of worthwhile material possessions. This little pile, along with memories good and bad in those he touched, is the sum total of his existence.

We took the stuff out and loaded it into the car and I returned to the porch to lock up. I had the key out and ready when I changed my mind. There was no thought involved; it was impulse, or maybe a sudden compulsion. I called to Kerry, "Hold on a minute, I'll be right back," and hurried inside and through the kitchen into the garage. I emptied the storage locker of everything except the wading boots and tackle box and spinning rods and reels. Loaded myself down with the rest so I wouldn't have to make a second trip and brought it out to the car.

Kerry didn't say anything; neither did I. There are some actions that don't need words. Or rationalization or justification, either.

9

Pam and Cliff Hoyt lived in Ross, one of the more affluent Marin County communities. Their house was a neo-Victorian with a half-wraparound front porch, shaded by conifers and spiky yew trees and one enormous magnolia in the middle of the lawn. A basketball hoop and net above the double garage doors pointed up the fact that they had a son. He was nine now and his name was Jason; he was Bobbie Jean's only grandchild.

All three Hoyts came out to greet Kerry and me when we arrived at two on Sunday afternoon. I was of two minds about being there; I wanted to talk to Bobbie Jean but I didn't really want to see again what Eberhardt had done to her. The visit had been Kerry's idea, the first stop of a two-part Sunday outing. Bobbie Jean and the Hoyts first, then a short drive south and some socializing and an early dinner with Kerry's mother, Cybil, at her seniors' complex in Larkspur. I'd let her talk me into it without much protest, as a payback for her accompanying me to Elizabeth Street yesterday. An hour or so with Bobbie Jean and her family was something to get through, but I liked Cybil now that she was independent and writing fiction again after a forty-year hiatus. She'd finished one novel and was into another, and it looked as though the first would be bought by one of the better New York publishers. The Eberhardts of the world make life seem bleak and futile; the Cybils are beacons of light, symbols of hope.

Cliff shook my hand and said again, as he had to Kerry on the phone, that he was glad we'd decided to stop by and that Bobbie Jean was eager to see us. His cheerfulness had a hollow ring. And Pam's smile was wan and thin, like one of those happy faces crookedly pasted on. Even Jason seemed subdued. All of which pretty much told me what to expect as we trooped in to where Bobbie Jean was waiting in what Pam called the sun room.

She was sitting in a lounge chair, an afghan tucked around her legs and a sweater over her shoulders despite the sun streaming in through tall rear windows. She didn't look any worse than she had at the funeral, but she didn't look any better, either. Drawn and tired-eyed, pain lines puckering the corners of her mouth, the flesh loose and wrinkled on her neck and under her chin. She'd put on rouge and lipstick, but it only called attention to the sickly pallor of her skin. The lingering impression I had was of an elderly hospital patient, propped and primped for the coming of callers.

But Kerry and I had our own masks on; we pretended she looked fine, made meaningless small talk designed to lift her spirits. I handed her the nonjunk mail I'd collected from the house yesterday; she barely glanced at it. I told her we'd pretty much finished going through both house and office, had separated out a few things we thought she might want.

They were in the car, Kerry said—would she like us to bring them in? No, not now. When we do give them to her, I thought, she won't want a single item. Wouldn't weaken as I had with the fishing gear. The part of her life that had included Eberhardt was as dead to her as he was, and understandably so. He'd hurt her far worse than any of us.

So then everyone except Jason sat around and drank coffee and didn't eat the carrot cake Pam had set out and made more small talk for forty interminable minutes. Eberhardt was such a presence in the room, though none of us mentioned his name, that his shade might have been sitting on one of the empty chairs, leaking ghost blood from the gaping wounds in his chest and back. I stood it as long as I could, finally got up and made excuses that were met with token protests from the Hoyts, silence from Bobbie Jean.

We were all on our feet except her when I said, "Bobbie Jean, I'd like to ask you a few questions before we leave."

"Questions?"

"Some things that turned up that puzzle me."

Faint smile. "Always the detective. Go ahead."

"Last Tuesday Eb deposited five hundred dollars in cash in his checking account. Do you have any idea where he got the money?"

". . . No. Five hundred dollars? Are you sure?"

"Deposit slip in his checkbook. He also wrote a check to somebody that same day for the same amount. No payee's name in the register. It wasn't to you?"

"No. I wrote him checks, not the other way around."

"That makes it even odder. Five hundred in cash is a lot of money, and for him to be writing a check for that much the day before he . . . Well, you see why it's bothersome."

She nodded. "I suppose it could have something to do with that liquor warehouse business."

"It's possible. Did he talk to you about the job he was doing for the O'Hanlon brothers?"

"No. He never said much about his work." She sighed, shifted position in the slow, careful way of people whose joints ache from arthritis. "If you want me to, I'll call the bank in the morning, find out if the check's been cashed."

"I'd appreciate it, Bobbie Jean. Just one more thing. Did you know Eb was seeing a psychologist, a man named Disney?"

Surprise flickered in her eyes, vanished and left them dull again. She said in a matching tone, "No, I didn't know that."

"There was a notation on his appointment calendar—two P.M. last Tuesday."

"He was a busy bee Tuesday, wasn't he." Still the dull voice, but bitterness was implicit in the words. "Have you spoken to the psychologist yet?"

"No, but I will."

"What can he tell you that you don't already know? He didn't do Eb any good, did he? Nobody could do him any good, least of all me. When a man wants to die as badly as he did, there's no way to change his mind. He's better off dead."

Pam said, "Mother . . ."

"It's the truth, dear. He's better off, I'm better off, you all are better off. He wanted to die and he's dead and that's the end of it."

Not as simple as that, Bobbie Jean, I thought. If it was, you'd be in far better shape right now. We'd all be in better shape, skipping right along with our lives. And none of us is.

But I kept all of that to myself. Yielded to Kerry's warning glance and tendered my good-byes. Each of us kissed Bobbie

Jean's cheek, and out we went with Cliff for company. Pam stayed with her mother.

Outside Cliff said, "I wish you hadn't asked all those questions. It still doesn't take much to upset her."

"I didn't mean for that to happen."

"I know you didn't, but good Lord, what importance can Eberhardt's actions his last few days possibly have?"

"None to anyone but me, I guess."

"That sounds as though you intend to keep investigating."

"For a while."

"Well, then, talk to Richard Disney or anyone but Bobbie Jean."

I said I wouldn't bother her anymore. I didn't add that I meant after she called the bank about that five-hundred-dollar check.

Richard Disney, Ph.D., practiced psychology out of a brown stucco-fronted Edwardian on Church a block off 24th Street. It was a Noe Valley address, not all that far from Eberhardt's house on Elizabeth—a private home that likely belonged to Disney and so allowed him the best of all possible commutes.

I rang the bell on the downstairs office door at a few minutes after nine Monday morning, on the theory that psychologists, like medical doctors and private detectives, were usually on the premises and not necessarily averse to seeing people earlier than their posted office hours. I was right in this case; the door buzzer went off almost immediately, giving me access into a carpeted foyer. At the end of a short hallway, a waiting room opened up. It was small, comfortable, like somebody's sparsely furnished living room. At the far end a desk was set between two closed doors; behind it sat a youngish woman with seal-brown hair and the kind of wide brown eyes that look enormous behind the lenses of glasses. Her glasses were rimmed in gold wire. A nameplate on her desk said she was Ms. Scott.

"Good morning," she said. "May I help you?"

"I'd like to see Dr. Disney, if he's in."

"He is, but he doesn't see clients until nine-thirty. And I'm afraid he has a full schedule today."

"I'm not a client, I'm here about one. A couple of minutes of his time is all I'm asking."

She didn't quite frown. "About one of our clients?"

"A man named Eberhardt."

"Eberhardt? The name isn't familiar."

"He had an appointment for two o'clock last Tuesday."

Ms. Scott opened an appointment book, flipped back a few pages. "Oh yes, now I remember. A Mr. Eberhardt did have an appointment but he called to cancel."

Which explained the cell phone call at 1:07 that afternoon. "What reason did he give?"

"I really can't say. May I ask why you're inquiring about him?"

"He was a friend." I gave her one of my business cards.

"Was?"

"He committed suicide last Wednesday morning. I'm trying to find out why."

She said automatically, "Oh, I'm sorry," and glanced at the card. "But I'm sure we can't help you."

"I understand about doctor-client confidentiality, but under the circumstances—"

"No, I'm afraid you don't understand. Mr. Eberhardt was not a client of Dr. Disney's."

"He wasn't? You mean the Tuesday appointment was his first?"

"That's correct. We never saw him."

"When did he make the appointment?"

"The day before. Monday."

"How? By phone?"

"I believe so, yes."

"Did he say how he came to pick Dr. Disney?"

"He was referred to us. Most of our clients come to us as referrals."

"Who referred him?"

"I can't give you that information."

"Can you at least tell me why he wanted to see the doctor?"

"No, I can't."

"Look, Ms. Scott, I knew the man for thirty-five years and it's important to me to find out why he killed himself. If you could just give me some idea—"

"That is out of the question."

Those words weren't hers; they came from a tall, spare party standing in the right-hand doorway. I hadn't heard him open the door, so he must have moved as quietly as a sneak thief. I wondered if he'd been standing behind it, maybe with it cracked open, eavesdropping on my conversation with Ms. Scott.

"Dr. Disney?"

"Yes." He was about forty and he might've been craggily good-looking in a Lincolnesque way if it hadn't been for the fact that he was missing most of his chin. The lower quarter of his face had an incomplete look, as if his chin and jawline had been made of some substance like wax that had melted and run before it had time to solidify. "I'll have to ask you to leave."

"If you heard what I said to Ms. Scott . . ."

He nodded stiffly. "Your reasons for coming here may be valid to you, but not to me. We do not give out information about my clients or my practice. Not for any reason or under any circumstances. Ms. Scott knows that, don't you, Ms. Scott?"

The rebuke had an arrogant edge, as if he were speaking to a naughty child. She took it without expression, and her "Yes, Doctor" was neutral, but her body language said she didn't like it much.

I was not going to get anywhere with Disney, so there was no point in arguing. I ignored him and said to the woman, "Thank you for your time, Ms. Scott," and smiled at her before I turned away. As I went along the hallway, the door back there shut behind the brain-picker with a lot less stealth than it had been opened.

I had the front door open and was starting out when I heard the rustle of clothing behind me, the quick muffled slide of shoes on the carpet. Ms. Scott, wearing a tight, defiant little smile. When she reached me, she said in an undertone, "Dr. Disney can be a pain in the ass," surprising me a little. "I'm thinking of quitting."

"Good jobs are hard to come by."

"Not if you're skilled at what you do. If I remember correctly, Mr. Eberhardt didn't give a specific reason for wanting to consult with the doctor. He seemed reluctant, as many new clients are. Last-minute cancelations are common in a psychologist's practice."

"Who referred him to Dr. Disney?"

"I believe it was Dr. Caslon at San Francisco General."

"Caslon. Attached to the staff there?"

"Yes."

"In what capacity?"

"He is an ER night resident."

"ER? You're sure?"

"Certainly."

"How did he know Eberhardt? How did he come to refer him?"

"I can't answer those questions."

"But Dr. Caslon can. Thanks again, Ms. Scott. And good luck, whatever you decide to do."

"I've already decided," she said, and showed me the tight smile again before she shut the door between us.

First thing at the office I called S.F. General and talked to a nurse in ER. She told me Dr. Caslon had Mondays and Tuesdays off; he would not be on shift again until Wednesday evening at seven. I asked for his home telephone number, saying it was important I get in touch with him. Wasted effort, as I'd known it would be. "We don't give out that information, sir," the nurse said in wintry tones. My thanks-and-good-bye went out into dead-line limbo.

I looked up Caslon in the white pages. No residential listing for anyone with that surname. Which meant either that Dr. Caslon had an unlisted home number or that he lived somewhere outside the city. I could have had Tamara run a computer check of the phone listings for all the nearby areas, except that she was busy on another skip-trace and this wasn't urgent enough to justify diverting her. Besides, for all I knew Dr. Caslon was unlisted wherever he lived and/or was away somewhere enjoying his days off; and in any case I'd have a better chance of getting information out of him if I spoke to him in person. He could wait until Wednesday night.

But that didn't stop me, once the noon hour rolled around and Tamara went out to lunch and left me by myself, from brooding over the connection between Eberhardt and a night resident physician in the emergency room at S.F. General. It wasn't likely to be personal; no Caslon listing in his address book, no mention of the name in any of his home or office papers that I recalled. Got drunk enough to hurt himself in some way that had landed him in ER one night? That seemed the most probable explanation, but then why hadn't somebody mentioned it? At least Bobbie Jean would've known . . .

I hadn't heard from her, so I called the Hoyts' number in Ross. Answering machine, but Bobbie Jean was there; when I identified myself after the tone, she cut off the machine and came on the line. Three-minute conversation, none of it enlightening and all of it difficult. Eberhardt's bank had no record of the five hundred dollar check being cashed, she said. And no, she didn't know anyone named Dr. Caslon; no, of course Eberhardt hadn't been injured in any way serious enough to send him to a hospital emergency room or she'd have known about it. I asked her if she would mind calling the bank again in two or three days; she said all right. But her tone, weary and resigned, said she wished I would please just drop the whole thing and leave her be.

I can't, Bobbie Jean, I thought as I hung up. I wish I could, for both our sakes, but I *can't*.

Tamara came back from lunch with the sandwich I'd asked her to get for me. I was chewing on half of it when the phone bell went off. And the conversation that ensued put an end to my appetite, knocked Eberhardt and Dr. Caslon and that mysterious five hundred dollars right out of my head.

A raspy male voice asked to speak to me, and I said he already was, and he said, "My name is Battle, Lieutenant Mike Battle, Sonoma County Sheriff's Department."

I didn't know anybody named Mike Battle. I said, "What can I do for you, Lieutenant?"

"Few questions about one Ira Erskine. Name familiar to you?"

"Yes. A recent client."

"How recent?"

"Last week."

"What sort of work did you do for him?"

"Well, that's confidential . . ."

"Under the circumstances you won't be violating client confidentiality by telling me. We'd appreciate your cooperation."

"Are you investigating some sort of felony involving Mr. Erskine?"

"Accident, the way it looks right now. But we don't have enough information yet to close the books on it."

"Serious accident?"

"As serious as they come. Fatal shooting. Early this morning at the Pinecrest Motel outside Healdsburg."

Uh-oh. "Who was shot?"

Battle said, "Ira Erskine. Apparently got careless cleaning a .38 Police Special in his room and blew off the back of his head."

10

I COOPERATED FULLY WITH SHERIFF'S Lieutenant Battle. It would have been foolish to do otherwise even if Ira Erskine was still among the living; cooperation with police agencies is vital to a private investigator if he wants to maintain friendly relations and avoid any official complaints to the State Board of Licenses. I gave him a quick rundown of Erskine's reasons for hiring me and the results of my investigation, and offered to fax him a copy of my report; he said that might be helpful and provided their fax number. Whatever Erskine had done with his copy of the report, it hadn't been among his effects in the motel room or in his rental car. What had been found that led Battle to me was my business card, tucked inside Erskine's folder of traveler's checks.

Even after the lieutenant rang off, I had some difficulty coming to terms with Erskine's sudden death. I hadn't liked him much, but I had empathized with his problems, and for him to die the way he had was a bitter nut to swallow. Cleaning a .38 Police Special with a round in firing position . . .

stupid as hell. But it happens more often than you might think, and the fact that a cleaning woman and two guests had heard the shot and within minutes found the body locked inside the ground-floor room seemed to support an accidental-shooting explanation. What gnawed at me was that Erskine had had the weapon in the first place. Why bring it with him from Santa Fe? Or if he'd gotten hold of it out here somehow, that made the situation even odder. Had he had some screwball idea of trying to force his ex-wife into returning to New Mexico with him? A man as in love with an ideal as he'd been was capable of something like that. Yet if she was any kind of human being, with even a shred of compassion or maternal feeling left in her, she'd have gone willingly to be with their dying son. From the impression of Sondra Nelson I'd been given by the hostess at Silver Creek Cellars, she was anything but cold-hearted.

Still . . . I'd told Erskine where to find her late Thursday afternoon. He'd had three full days to contact her, tell her about the boy. So why had he still been at a Healdsburg motel this morning unless she'd turned him down flat? And not just hanging around there, waiting, but cleaning that .38 Police Special?

Strange dude, Tamara had called him. No argument there. Well, maybe the .38 hadn't had any direct connection to his reunion with his ex-wife. Maybe he'd been one of these paranoid gun nuts who see menace lurking everywhere they go and can't travel ten miles without packing heat for protection. And San Francisco, after all, as everybody east of Reno knows to be gospel fact, is a wicked, wicked city.

I asked Tamara to fax a copy of the Erskine report to Lieutenant Battle, and while she did that she offered her take on the situation. Which was suicide. Sondra Nelson had blown him off; refused to go back to Santa Fe to be with their son, given him no hope of reconciliation. And he'd been "whacked out" enough to take himself out. I said I didn't buy it, but that was because I'd had enough of people ending their own lives with handguns; I didn't want to deal with the issue even in theory. It was possible, though. At this stage anything was possible.

Ira Erskine was dead, that was all anybody knew for sure. And his son was still dying alone back in Santa Fe. Sondra Nelson's past had caught up with her with a vengeance. Yes, and I was more than a little responsible.

Feelings of guilt began to build in me, to the point where I considered contacting her and expressing my regrets. But I didn't give in to the urge; I was the last person she'd want to talk to, now or ever. In a few days I could call Battle, get a follow-up on Erskine's death and find out what Sondra Nelson's plans were regarding her son. Otherwise I was out of a tragic and difficult situation and I'd be smart to keep it that way.

Wrong.

I wasn't out of it. Not by a damn sight.

Sheriff's Lieutenant Battle called again early Tuesday morning. He said without preamble, "The Erskine shooting. It's not as cut and dried as I thought. There're inconsistencies." His tone put me on alert; it was more official-sounding today. "Conflicting information that needs clarifying."

"How can I help? I told you everything I know yesterday—"

"I'd prefer we talk in person this time, if it's all the same to you. What's your schedule like today? Can you free up time to come to Santa Rosa?"

"I think so. What's convenient for you?"

"Say one o'clock. Our offices are at six hundred Administration Drive. You know where that is?"

"I've been to the courthouse."

"One o'clock," he said, and left me sitting there holding the receiver and thinking, *What the hell?*

Half a century ago, Santa Rosa—fifty-some miles due north of San Francisco—was a sleepy little town with a population of under twenty thousand, built close around the then two-lane Highway 101. Alfred Hitchcock considered it such a perfect example of prewar small-town America that he picked it for the location shooting of one of his best films, *Shadow of a Doubt*. Even twenty-five years ago its growth rate was relatively slow and it retained much of its quiet, homegrown ambiance. Since the early seventies, though, spurred on by high birth rates and thousands of new residents pouring into California every year, not to mention that old debbil greed, hordes of real estate developers descended on Sonoma County and have since turned a few million acres of open farmland and rolling wooded hills into look-alike housing tracts and shopping centers and "luxurious hillside homes with spectacular views." The perfect example of small-town America has evolved into the perfect example of late-twentieth-century urban and suburban sprawl. Santa Rosa's population has ballooned to 150,000 and shows no sign of leveling off, and right along with its rampant growth, the burgeoning new city has been plagued by the usual assortment of urban social ills: ghettoization of poorer neighborhoods, homelessness, widespread drug and gang activity, and a steady upsurge in violent crime.

The newish complex built around Administration Drive, off the freeway north of downtown, was an inevitable result of the urbanization of Santa Rosa and population increases throughout Sonoma County. All of the county's administrative buildings and offices are located there, in an area that covers several acres. There are parking facilities for a few thousand cars, but I couldn't find a spot anywhere within a short hike of the courthouse and sheriff's offices. I had to walk nearly half a mile from where I finally deposited the car. Not that I minded the exercise but Battle's second call had put an edginess in me and the sooner I found out what was back of it, the better I'd feel. Maybe.

The parking hunt and the walk made me ten minutes late. Battle didn't seem bothered; he waved away my apology, told me to have a seat, and spent a few seconds taking my measure while I did the same with him. His office was not much larger than a cubicle and the two of us pretty much filled it; he was a couple of inches taller and fifty pounds heavier than me, which made him a very big man. Forty-some years of living and somewhere around half that number in law enforcement had lined and toughened his face, and his eyes, dark brown under heavy brows and a low-hanging shock of iron-gray hair, said that he couldn't be pushed or fooled and you'd be well advised not to try to do either.

"I did some checking on you," he said. "You've got a rep for honesty, so I'm assuming everything you told me yesterday is factual. The story Erskine handed you, the nature and substance of your investigation."

"It's factual. I wouldn't have any reason to lie or withhold information."

"But evidently Erskine did."

"You mean he lied to me?"

"That's right."

"For instance?"

"The terminally ill son back in Santa Fe."

". . . The boy's not dying of leukemia?"

"There is no boy," Battle said. "No son, no living children. His only child was a little girl and she died in infancy five years ago. Crib death, age five months."

I sat there with my mouth hanging open a little. "His ex-wife?"

"She's real enough. The mother of the baby that died. But if she was ever a drug addict, the Santa Fe police have no record of any arrests, and a woman at the Salishan Gallery who knew her disputes it. She was never in a rehab center in New Mexico."

"The disappearance three years ago . . . ?"

"Oh, she left Santa Fe after a divorce and settlement, but it was four years ago, not three. From there she went to Taos for a while, not Albuquerque. Then she moved back to Chicago, where she was born, and then to St. Louis, Phoenix, and finally out here about three years ago. In St. Louis she had her name legally changed to Sondra Nelson."

"She tell you all that?"

"Yesterday afternoon, at James Woolfox's ranch. Funny thing is, I could've saved myself the trip. She was right here at the courthouse until one-thirty. Jury duty. So she couldn't have had any direct involvement in the shooting. Erskine died at approximately 7:40 A.M., and she was already in the jury room by then. Jury Commissioner's office verified it."

I was silent for a little time, working to sort out and reslot all the new information he was feeding me. "Before she settled in the Alexander Valley, why did she move around so much?"

"Same reason she changed her name. To keep Erskine from finding her."

"Afraid of him?"

"Scared to death."

"Jesus, don't tell me he was a wife-stalker?"

"Just what he was, according to her. Abused her before the baby's death, even more afterward. She tried to leave him a couple of times; he dragged her back. Love-hate thing on his part, and violent both ways. Last time he beat her up she had to be hospitalized and that's when she filed for divorce. He kept after her, she got a restraining order and moved to Taos. He went up there and threatened to kill her. The old story—'If I can't have you, nobody can.' That was when she started running in earnest."

"And I found her for him. Bought that sob story of his without checking any damn part of it." I smacked the heels of my palms together, hard enough to hurt. "Stupid. Stupid! There were signs . . . I should've recognized them for what they were."

"What signs?"

"He was so intense. Obsessive. And the way he reacted when I found her, some things he said that I ignored or misinterpreted—Christ. It never even occurred to me he might be stalking her."

"Don't beat yourself up," Battle said. "Everybody makes mistakes in judgment. Besides, he's the one who's dead, not her."

"He must've seen her, talked to her. What happened?"

"Showed up at the winery Friday morning. She nearly had a hemorrhage. After four years she figured she was safe."

"Yeah."

"No threats then. Charm and pleas—told her how good she looked, how much he still loved her and wanted her back. He wouldn't leave. Then Woolfox got into it."

"And?"

"Some harsh words between the two men, that's all. Erskine left, but an hour later he started calling up the winery. She wouldn't talk to him. So that night he began pestering Gail Kendall, the winery chemist. Found out somehow she was his ex's best friend and the two of them had roomed together until six weeks ago, when Nelson moved out to Woolfox's ranch. Erskine got wind of that, too. On Saturday afternoon he showed up at the ranch."

"With or without the Police Special?"

"If he had it with him, he didn't flash it," Battle said. "Verbal threats only, but pretty strong ones. He wouldn't leave until Woolfox told his housekeeper to phone us. But he was back again on Sunday, at the ranch and winery both—not that it did him any good. Woolfox and Nelson spent Saturday night and Sunday with a friend in the Napa Valley. Kendall was invited along because they were afraid Erskine would continue to harass her."

"And Monday morning Erskine turns up dead of a gunshot wound. End of threat. Convenient."

"Coincidences happen. And disturbed people do foolish things."

"So you're satisfied the shooting was accidental?"

"Satisfied? No, not yet. That's one of the reasons you're here. It could've been suicide; stalkers are prone to taking that way out. But seldom until they've killed the woman first. That's their whole focus, either getting her to come back to them or killing her if she refuses. Why go to all the trouble to track her down and then take no for a quick answer and blow himself away? Doesn't fit the psychological profile."

"No, it doesn't," I agreed.

"Homicide's more likely, but the circumstances seem to rule it out. He was alone in the room, the door and windows all locked tight. Mexican maid and two guests heard the shot, and the male guest, a man named Doyle, convinced the maid to use her passkey. He swears they were inside Erskine's room within five minutes. And that he didn't hear anything inside after the shot, or see anything suspicious in the vicinity."

"Pretty convincing, all right."

"And that's not all," Battle said. "The locals who had reason to want Erskine dead all have solid alibis. Sondra Nelson was here at the courthouse on jury duty, like I said. Woolfox was still in the Napa Valley; not only his friend but the friend's wife and a grown daughter verify it. Gail Kendall went back home Sunday night—she lives in the hills near Geyserville—and her car had a dead battery when she got up Monday morning. She called Triple A to come out and jump it for her. The tow-truck driver confirms time and place."

"One of the three could've hired it done," I said.

"Anything's possible. But where would respectable citizens find a paid assassin on short notice? And even if one could be found, why would he go to a lot of trouble to arrange a fake shooting accident in a motel room? There are a few hundred better, safer ways and places."

I nodded. "Yet you're still not quite ready to close it out as accidental. How come?"

"You've cleared up some of the inconsistencies, but there're still loose ends. And the fact of Erskine turning up dead so soon after threatening his ex-wife. Convenient coincidences happen, but that doesn't mean I like them. Anything more you can tell me?"

"I don't think so. I've got a few questions, though. Things that occurred to me while we've been talking."

"Go ahead."

"How much corroboration have you got that Erskine was an abuser and a stalker?"

"Enough. The woman at the Salishan Gallery in Santa Fe confirmed the abuse; so did hospital records. We verified the restraining order and three complaints by Janice Erskine on file with the Santa Fe and Taos police. And both Woolfox and his housekeeper were witnesses when Erskine threatened her life at the ranch on Saturday."

"Did Woolfox know about Erskine before he showed up? Or did she keep her past a secret from him?"

"Told him everything when they got engaged." Battle paused and then said mildly, "You wouldn't be trying to build a scenario that'll help ease your conscience, would you?"

"No way. I screwed up and I accept full responsibility. I'm going to feel lousy about it for a long time."

He watched me awhile, then shrugged and said, "Yeah, well, live and learn. Anyhow, there's no question that she was terrified of Erskine. It was in her voice and her eyes the whole time I talked to her. He was stalking her, and the odds are he'd have harmed her eventually, or tried to. My job is to make sure a case is what it seems to be before I wrap it up, but I hope like hell this one *was* an accidental shooting. Nice justice in a stalker getting careless and blowing himself away *before* he harms the woman."

"Wouldn't make me unhappy, either," I said. "Sounds like she's had a rough time."

"Too damn rough. She seems decent—I liked her."

"She still on jury duty, or did they let her off?"

"Empaneled for a gang-rape trial, called but not seated. Obligation completed."

"One more question, Lieutenant?"

"Ask it."

"Did she send a postcard to an old friend in Santa Fe, or was that another of Erskine's lies?"

"Lie. She swears she's had no contact with anyone in Santa Fe since she left Taos. Wouldn't have dared risk writing a postcard or letter, or making a phone call, or even setting foot back in New Mexico."

"Then how did he track her to this area?"

"He didn't tell her and she doesn't have any idea."

"Well, if it was through another private detective, he or she is a hell of a lot smarter than me."

"How so?"

"Figured out what Erskine was up to and refused to have anything more to do with him. Otherwise, he wouldn't have needed me."

"How'd he happen to pick you, anyhow?"

"Referral list from an agency in Santa Fe. That's what he told my assistant."

"Which agency?"

"Patterson."

"You know them?"

"Yes. Reputable firm. I handled a split-fee investigation for them a few years ago. He probably did get a referral list from them. Either they did work for him, or he paid them a small consultancy fee."

"I'll check, see if they can tell me something I don't already know." Battle got to his feet. "Well, I think that's it for now. I have your card, here's one of mine. Call me if you think of anything else."

I said I would, and that should have been the end of my involvement in the matter. But it wasn't, not just yet.

Ira Erskine had made a fool out of me, a burden compounded by what I'd done to Sondra Nelson—and James Woolfox and Gail Kendall—by turning a psychopath loose on her without even a whisper of advance warning. The guilt I felt today was twice as strong as yesterday's, too strong to ignore. I couldn't just fade away, forget it all as if it had never happened; I'm not made that way. I had to have some sort of closure in this case, just as I needed one in Eberhardt's suicide. And that meant facing her, owning up—not because I wanted her forgiveness, but because it was the only way I could begin to forgive myself.

11

CLOUDS WERE FORMING A LOW, DARK overcast and there was a sharp ground-hugging wind when I reached the junction of Alexander Valley Road and Highway 128. It was only two-thirty but shadows were already long in the folds and hollows of the hills, among the thicker stands of oaks that flanked 128. Rain later on, I thought. Maybe even a good-size storm. I could smell the ozone in the air even with the windows tightly shut.

The public parking area at Silver Creek Cellars was deserted. For the most part, wine-tasting is a fair-weather, weekend pursuit. The tasting room was still open, though; small wineries can't afford to pander to the vagaries of weather or to make blanket assumptions about human nature. I parked as close as I could to the smaller stone building and let the wind hurry me inside.

The tasting room had two occupants, the blond hostess I'd talked to last Thursday and the heavyset, red-haired woman who'd complained about too much residual sugar in one of the fermenting vats. They were having a conversation in a small office behind the counter. The blonde noticed me as I entered, came out smiling and saying "Welcome to—" Recognition put an abrupt end to both the greeting and the smile. "Oh," she said in chilly tones, "it's you again. The liar."

"Me again."

"You have a lot of nerve coming back here."

"I know it. Is Sondra Nelson—"

"I'm not going to talk to you," she said, "not after what you did, the way you lied to me. Why don't you go away? You're not wanted at Silver Creek."

"Look, miss—"

"What's going on, Paula?" That from the redhead, standing in the office doorway. She moved forward to join the other woman and I had my first good look at Gail Kendall. A nametag pinned above the pocket of her white smock read "Gail," so I assumed that was who she was. Late thirties, solid and big-boned rather than overweight, with a wedge-shaped chin and a generous mouth. Homely, but in an appealing way. The old saw about opposites attracting sometimes applies to same-sex friendships, too: she was nothing at all like the woman in Ira Erskine's photographs.

The blonde, Paula, said, "He's that detective, the one who found Sandy for her pig of an ex-husband."

The look Gail Kendall fixed on me would have clabbered milk. Except that in her anger-hot eyes I was a different and much darker substance, the kind you detour around when you spot it dirtying the ground. "What the hell do *you* want?"

"To see Sondra Nelson. Or James Woolfox, if she's not here."

"Why?"

"I'd rather tell her personally."

"More trouble, is that it?"

"No, ma'am. Not from me."

"You know what you almost did, siccing that son-of-a-bitch on Sandy? You have any idea?"

"I do now. I didn't last Thursday."

"That's no excuse. Couldn't you see what he was? Or didn't you care?"

"I wouldn't be here if I didn't care. And yes, I should've seen what he was but I didn't."

"Why didn't you at least talk to her, give her some warning? What right does a man like you have to poke into people's lives without them knowing anything about it?"

"I made a mistake, Ms. Kendall, and I'm sorry for it."

"How do you know my name?"

"Sheriff's Lieutenant Battle."

She made a spitting mouth. "I suppose he's sorry, too. Everybody's so damn sorry. You think that makes it all right, being sorry?"

"No. But it's all I have to offer."

"Leave Sandy and Jim alone. You've caused them enough grief."

"No more grief, just a few minutes of her time, or his. Is either of them here?"

"No."

"At his ranch?"

"They're not anywhere in the valley right now, thanks to you. Not anywhere in the state."

"Come on, Ms. Kendall. The lieutenant wouldn't have let them leave the county, much less the state, with his investigation still open."

". . . Did he tell you that? He's still investigating?"

"Yes."

"Why, for God's sake? Erskine shot himself. It was an accident, how could it be anything else?"

"Nobody's saying it's anything else."

"Then why isn't the goddamn subject closed?"

"I think you'd better ask him."

"I will, if he comes here again. Sandy's had enough, more than one person can take. Enough, you hear me?" She shook an angry finger a couple of inches from my nose. "Get off this property or I'll call some of the workers and have them throw you off. Now!"

I said mildly, "That's quite a temper you have."

"When I'm provoked. Keep standing there and provoking me and see what happens."

"No, thanks. I'll be going."

"And don't come back. Ever."

Hard-shell woman, I thought as I left the building. Full of fire when it comes to people she cares about. That was admirable, but I couldn't help wondering how far she'd go to protect a friend. How explosive her temper was when she was really provoked.

At the crossroads store upvalley I had a look into the Sonoma County phone book. Erskine had managed without much difficulty to find out where James Woolfox lived, which probably meant that Woolfox had a listed number and address. Right: 10116 Chalk Hill Road. I put gas in the car, asked the store clerk for directions to Chalk Hill Road—it was back the way I'd come, past Silver Creek Cellars—and pulled out again onto Highway 128.

Number 10116 was about three miles along Chalk Hill's twisty course. An asphalt drive led in under a wrought-iron arch set into pillars, the words "JSW RANCH" in the center of the arch. The drive hooked around the brow of a low hill planted in grapevines; more vineyards stretched away on the opposite side. A quarter of a mile in, the vineyards ended and pastureland opened up—rough terrain full of rises and dips, carpeted in bunch grass and spotted with craggy outcrops, ancient oaks, several grazing horses. Beautiful setting, unspoiled by the ranch buildings arranged in the lee of the hill in such a fashion that they seemed almost part of the landscape. Aspens flanked the drive leading in to the ranchyard and more oaks shaded house, stables, and other outbuildings. Judging from this place and the winery, James Woolfox had both taste and an affinity for nature.

The house was an old two-story frame, brightly whitewashed and trimmed out in dark greens and browns that matched the oak colors. An arbored area the size of a football field extended out in front and to one side; grapevines grew thickly over its trellised roof and supports. Underneath was a garden and a lot of wrought-iron outdoor furniture, and on one of the benches a man sat alone, bundled in a heavy wool jacket. He stayed put, watching my approach, until I reached the end of the drive where it widened out into a parking area. Then he stood and came out to meet me.

Average size, average features enhanced by a symmetrical, silvering beard neatly barbered. Hair darker, thick and wind-tangled. Crowding fifty, but youthful looking and in good shape. His face was drawn, the eyes sad and carrying heavy baggage underneath.

"Mr. Woolfox?"

"That's right." Hoarse voice, as if he had a sore throat or incipient laryngitis. I had the impression he was one of these self-contained, quiet men who speak only when they have something to say—and that he'd had to do a lot more talking than he was used to the past couple of days. "Which breed are you?"

"I'm sorry . . . breed?"

"Newspaper, TV, radio."

"Oh, I see. I'm not a reporter, Mr. Woolfox."

"No? Then—?"

"But I am here about Ira Erskine," I said. "I have some things to say to you and your fiancée."

He'd stiffened a little. "Things?"

"I'm the detective Erskine hired, the man who found Ms. Nelson for him."

I watched his face harden, set tight. But he remained silent for half a minute or so, staring at me without blinking. The wind gusted around us, cold and moany, rattling the tree branches and arbor vines. It was no more frigid than Woolfox's stare.

He said finally, "Say what you came to and get off my land."

"I'd like Ms. Nelson to hear it, too. Is she here?"

"She's resting. I won't disturb her, not for you."

"It'll only take a couple of minutes—"

"No."

"All right." The wind, gusting again, made me say then, "Can we at least talk inside? It's pretty cold out here."

"You're not welcome in my house."

"The porch, or inside my car? Out of the wind."

The porch suited him; he said as much and led me up there. It girdled the ground floor on two sides, the part facing the open pastureland enclosed in glass. Woolfox stopped as soon as we were protected by the glass and turned to face me again.

"I'm listening," he said.

I said, "It wasn't easy for me to come here like this, but I felt I owed it to you and Ms. Nelson. Myself, too. I want you both to know I had no idea Erskine was stalking her. If

I had I'd've notified the authorities immediately. He told me a pack of plausible lies about having a son in Santa Fe who was dying of leukemia, wanting to locate his ex-wife to give her the news about the boy. I swallowed his story whole. That's not an excuse; I don't have any excuses to make. I should've checked on him and I didn't. At least I should have talked to your fiancée before I told Erskine where to find her and I didn't do that, either. I can't undo the damage. All I can do is tell you and her I'm sorry."

"Cold comfort," Woolfox said.

"I know it. But cold comfort is better than none at all."

"Is it?"

"I'd like to think so."

"The last honorable man."

"You don't strike me as someone who sneers at honor, Mr. Woolfox."

The long, silent stare again. To one side of him I thought I saw the curtain move at an inside window, the blurred shapes of head and arm and shoulder behind it. A second later, the shapes were gone and the curtain hung motionless again.

Woolfox blinked, let breath hiss out between his teeth; some of the rigidity seemed to leave his body, and along with it, some of his hostility. He said, "I can't forgive you. Your carelessness could have brought harm to a woman I love deeply."

"Forgiveness isn't an issue," I said.

"No, I suppose not. You were right before, I'm not a man who sneers at honor. But for you to come here like this—"

He broke off, glancing past me. That and the whisper of footsteps turned me sideways. A woman had come out through the front door and was approaching us in stiff, deliberate strides. Her age and the short, brown curly hair would have identified her even if there hadn't been a strong resemblance to the photographs of Janice Durian Erskine. The first thing that struck me about Sondra Nelson in the flesh was how much she'd matured in five years, how much more attractive at thirty-something she was despite the effects of fear and stress. In her twenties her near-beauty had been the fragile kind; over the past few years it had solidified and strengthened, as if a fine steel mesh had been added in layers beneath the skin. Janice Erskine would have crumbled and run scared again as soon as her former husband showed up; Sondra Nelson was all through running and had been for some time.

Woolfox said, "You shouldn't be out here without a coat," and stepped past me to her side. "You shouldn't have come outside at all."

She smiled tenderly at him. "This sweater's warm enough." The sweater was a bulky-knit, black like the slacks she wore; but it was a safe bet the color choice had nothing to do with mourning. Her crimson smile flattened out before she said to me, "I overheard part of what you were saying a minute ago."

"I meant every word, Ms. Nelson."

"I'm sure you did. I can't forgive you any more than Jim can, but I don't hold you responsible. Ira's dead, that part of my life is over—it's all that matters."

"For your sake I'm glad it turned out that way. But the fact is, I hold myself responsible."

"We all suffer for our sins."

"Some of us more than others."

"Yes. Before you go, will you answer two questions for me?"

"Of course, if I can."

"How did you find me? The sheriff's lieutenant wasn't clear about that and I'd like to know. Something to do with the Silver Creek label . . . ?"

I explained about the photographs, Ms. Weissman, the Salishan Gallery connection.

"That damn label," Woolfox said. "I should never have insisted you design it."

"You didn't know about Ira then, sweet."

"You should've told me then, instead of letting me push you into doing the design."

"I wasn't sure of us or myself two years ago. I did the label to please you, because you wanted it so badly. And to please myself, because I was ready to paint again. It seemed safe enough. A small winery, estate-bottled vintages mostly distributed in California . . . and Ira neither drank nor had any interest in wine. If it hadn't been for . . ."

She let the rest of it trail off, so I finished it for her. "If it hadn't been for me, chances are he'd never have found you that way."

"You must be a very good detective," she said.

"Not in this case."

"Well." She asked then, "When were you sure Sandy Nelson and Janice Erskine were the same person . . . last Thursday after you'd been to the winery, was it?"

"Yes."

"Why didn't you come back on Friday and talk to me? That's the second thing I'd like to know. Why didn't you at least call and give me a chance to tell you my side before you went to Ira?"

"I don't have a defensible answer, Ms. Nelson. I should have talked to you first, no question. All I can say is that I had some personal matters on my mind that may have clouded my judgment. Anyhow, I still believed Erskine's lies about a son dying of leukemia. It didn't seem necessary at the time to contact you myself."

"And of course Ira asked you not to."

"Yes, but that's not an acceptable excuse, either."

She looked away, out over the wind-rippled landscape. "He was always such a brilliantly devious liar when he wanted something badly enough. I've never known anyone who could manufacture lies the way Ira could on the spur of the moment. Or who could hate as intensely as he hated. He claimed to still love me, but he really didn't, you know. Love turned to hate the day Karen died, but both emotions were so violent even I couldn't tell the difference right away."

"Karen . . . your daughter?"

She nodded. Old pain moved like a current behind her eyes, beneath the surfaces of her face. "A crib death, one of those terrible tragedies no one can prevent. But Ira blamed me. Blamed me and beat me . . ." Headshake. Slow, labored breath. Then, "He would have killed me eventually, no matter what I said or did. It was only a matter of time."

Woolfox said, "He was a monster," and tightened his protective embrace with enough force to make her wince.

"A monster is exactly what he was."

"But he'll never hurt you again. No one will ever hurt you as long as I'm alive."

She favored him with another smile and he kissed her cheek. Very much in love, those two; genuinely deep and abiding affection can't be feigned or mistaken. It was the kind of closeness Kerry and I felt toward each other. I'd kill to protect her—almost had once, not long ago—and I was pretty sure she'd do the same for me. Woolfox and Nelson, too?

As far as they were concerned I was already gone, but I

mumbled something about wishing her peace and happiness, repeated how sorry I was—a run-on exit line that I ought to've swallowed instead—and left them clinging to each other. They were already inside out of the cold by the time I finished turning the car around.

Now it was a closed case for me, I thought as I drove out to Chalk Hill Road. I'd done my penance, made my lame apologies, and they could proceed with their marriage and their winemaking and their life together in rustic Alexander Valley, and I could get on with my work and my life and try to profit from the foolish mistakes I'd made.

Right?

Sure, right.

So why did I feel dissatisfied and vaguely cheated, as though I'd run into new layers of deception—and more illusion—this afternoon? And why did I have a hunch I wasn't quite rid of the Erskine case after all and that it wasn't over for any of the principals except Erskine himself?

12

A FAIRLY ROUTINE BACKGROUND CHECK kept Tamara and me busy all of Wednesday morning and into early afternoon. The daughter of a well-off Hillsborough widow had met a man on a Mexican cruise and become engaged to him by the time the cruise ship docked again in L.A., and the widow was concerned that he might be a fortune hunter; she went to her lawyer and he called me. The check turned up some interesting information about the boyfriend's past, including one arrest and conviction in Galveston, Texas, for bilking a woman of forty thousand dollars in a real estate investment scam. The lawyer was pleased to hear my report; the widow would be pleased to hear it. The daughter wouldn't be, but she'd get over it and thank her mother someday. And I'd be pleased when I received the check to cover my fee. The only loser was the con artist, which was as it should be, and why the hell couldn't all my investigations turn out to have such simple happy endings?

Shortly before two I had a call from the claims adjustor

at one of the small insurance companies I work for now and then. Would I be able to come in this afternoon for a brief conference concerning a personal injury claim the company considered suspect? I would. We made an appointment for two-thirty, which gave me just enough time to drive downtown to the insurer's offices on lower Market, garage the car, and allow myself to be shot upward fourteen floors in a box not much larger than the one Eberhardt had been planted in. Elevators have a claustrophobic effect on me. God forbid I should ever find myself trapped in one between floors for any length of time; the ordeal would probably reduce me to a bag of gibbering clay.

The personal injury claim was suspect, all right. A thirty-three-year-old man who slips and falls in the produce section of a supermarket and claims to have suffered such grievous injuries as recurrent back spasms, impaired use of his left leg, and a groin pull so severe he is unable to sit comfortably in any kind of chair, and whose attorney is whoring after a settlement of two hundred thousand dollars in lieu of a million-dollar lawsuit against the supermarket chain, is either the world's most fragile human being or a fraud trying to happen big-time. I told the adjustor I'd see if I could get his employers off the hook, we settled on my usual fee, and I was out of there.

It was three-oh-five when I exited the building. Last night's rain had turned into a misty overcast with just enough moisture to keep a sheen of wetness on the sidewalks. And as I made my slippery way to the garage, it occurred to me that Embarcadero Center was only a few short blocks away. Great Western Insurance had its offices in one of the Center's high-rises, and among GWI's rabbit warren of glass-walled cubicles was the large one in which Barney Rivera held sway. Well? I was going to have to see him sooner or later, whether he liked it or not. Might as well be sooner, and at my convenience instead of his.

I changed direction, hoofed it over there, put myself into another elevator and let it hurl me like an object in a pneumatic tube twenty-nine floors above the city streets. When I popped out, I was facing a young male receptionist, who treated me to a bored look and asked what, please, he could do for me. I said Barney Rivera and offered my name; he wanted to know if I had an appointment; I said no, and he told me to have a seat, he'd see if Mr. Rivera was available. Ritual scene. I wondered, as I waited, how many times I'd played it over the past thirty years, mouthing the same dialogue or any number of dull variations, with a legion of faceless receptionists, secretaries, and factotums of both genders. Thinking about it, I decided I understood exactly what T. S. Eliot had meant with his oft-quoted line about measuring out his life in coffee spoons.

Pretty soon the receptionist replaced the handset on his switchboard unit and said to me in his bored voice, "Mr. Rivera is sorry, he can't see you today. He's very busy."

"Is that right?"

"Yes, sir. Would you care to make an appointment?"

"I don't think so," I said. I stood up and headed not for the elevator but for the door that led into the rabbit warren.

The receptionist was caught off guard; visitors were not supposed to act in such aggressive fashion. He gawped at me and said, "Wait a minute, sir, you can't—"

I said, "Yes, I can," and opened the door and went on through. I'd been in the warren enough times over the years; I knew where Rivera's cubicle was and how to get there through the maze. His double-size glass office had a door, which told you right away how important he was in GWI's scheme of things. I yanked it open, walked inside, and banged it shut behind me.

"I guess you're seeing me after all," I said.

He was probably surprised, but he didn't show it; he seldom showed much of what was going on inside his head, which made him a good poker player and a bad risk for personal intimacy. He peered up at me from behind his desk, his tubby little body so dwarfed by it that he looked like a doe-eyed, mop-headed kid playing executive. Women, for some insane reason, found him cute and cuddly and either wanted to mother him or screw his brains out; in all the years I'd known him, he had never lacked for female companionship. There had been a time, pre-Kerry, when I'd been a touch jealous of the man. Now his success with women and the careless way he treated his conquests were just two more reasons to dislike him.

He said, "What do you think—" and then broke off because the door opened and the receptionist poked his head inside. "I'm sorry Mr. Rivera he just barged in do you want me to call security?" all in a breathless rush. Barney said no, it was all right, he'd handle it, and the kid retreated and closed the door so softly I didn't even hear it click.

Rivera reached out to the dish on his desk and popped a peppermint before he finished what he'd started to say to me. "What do you think this macho act is going to buy you?"

"Some cleared air. I don't like being given the runaround."

"And I don't like former friends showing up unannounced."

"Former friends. Right. Just like that, huh?"

"You treated Eberhardt like shit," he said.

"Oh, sure. And he treated me like royalty?"

"You know what I mean."

"Four years and not a word from him, and then he calls up out of the blue, no explanation, and I'm supposed to drop everything and rush to his aid?"

"You could've talked to him, at least."

"I was two hundred and fifty miles away, for Christ's sake, and jammed up in that Sentinels mess. I had no idea he was in trouble, any kind of trouble. Nobody told me. Not Bobbie Jean and sure as hell not you."

"I didn't know it was as bad as it was until two weeks ago," Rivera said, "right before I phoned your office the first time. You didn't bother to get back to me and you were still in town then. Your secretary said so."

"Tamara's my assistant, not my secretary. And you told her it was personal and nothing urgent."

"The hell I did. Personal, yes, but I didn't say it wasn't urgent."

"Did you say it *was*?"

"I don't remember."

"Well, maybe she misunderstood. Or maybe she took it for granted because you didn't tell her otherwise."

"Passing the buck?" he said snottily.

"No!"

"Either way, you didn't return the call. My second one, either."

"I was up in Creekside by then and you still didn't tell Tamara what you were calling about."

"It wasn't her business. I told her personal. She told you personal, didn't she?" When I didn't answer, he reached for another peppermint. Outwardly he seemed his usual calm, unruffled self, but there was a kind of savagery in the way he was looking at me—a hint of the cruel streak that ran deep and dark in him. "You used to be somebody who returned personal calls right away."

"I used to have friends named Eberhardt and Rivera, too. Friends who gave as well as took." I moved forward and leaned on a corner of his desk with both hands, more to keep him from seeing that the hands weren't quite steady than for any other reason. "I couldn't have saved him, can't you see that? You couldn't stop him from killing himself, Bobbie Jean couldn't, how was I supposed to after four years?"

"That's not the point," he said. "The point is, you didn't even try."

"This is crazy, this whole conversation. We're like a couple of guys trying to shoot each other down through a bulletproof glass wall."

"You're the one who came busting in here."

"Bang. Now it's my turn again, right?" I leaned closer, my body bowed across his desk and my face only about a foot from his. He didn't pull back; whatever else he was, he wasn't a man who could be intimidated. "No more bullshit, Barney. What happened two weeks ago with you and Eberhardt?"

It was a few tense beats before he answered. His jaws moved, crunching on the peppermint; his breath smelled like a scratch-and-sniff add for Brach's. He swallowed before he said, "I called him at his office to offer him a claims investigation. Eleven o'clock in the morning. He was so drunk I could barely understand him."

"What day was that?"

"Same day as my first call to you."

"Monday?"

"You know it was. Monday morning."

"And?"

"And what?"

"Come on, man. You must've known he was drinking heavily before that. You didn't call me just because he was drunk at 11 A.M."

"He mumbled something about being ready to throw in the towel. I thought he meant quit the detective racket, but when I asked him he said no, he might as well check out for good. I figured it was the booze talking—I tried to kid him out of it. He wouldn't kid. He said he was afraid he'd go too far, and even if he didn't, it was too late for him to come back."

"Go too far? Meaning what?"

"I don't know. I couldn't get a coherent answer out of him. He mumbled some more and then hung up. Concerned me enough to want to talk to you about it, get your input. My mistake."

"Put the frigging needle away, Barney. Second time you called was Wednesday. Follow-up, or had you talked to him again?"

"Both. He called me Tuesday afternoon."

"Drunk or sober?"

"Sober. Mostly, anyway. Wanted to apologize, he said. Hadn't meant to lay all his crap on me but he was at the end of his rope. Didn't see much point in trying to hang on anymore. I asked him flat out if he was seriously thinking about doing away with himself. Took him a while to answer. Then he said, 'Don't be surprised if you hear I ate my gun.' "

"Those exact words?"

"That's right. And he hung up again before I could say anything else."

"What'd you do about it besides call my office again?"

"What you didn't do," he said. "Kept trying to get in

touch with him. He wasn't at his office any of the times I phoned, or home when I called there or when I drove out Friday night after work. I left messages on his machine and with Bobbie Jean, but like you, he never got back to me."

"You didn't leave messages after Friday night. You see or talk to him over the weekend, or Monday or Tuesday?"

"No, I told you, he never got back to me."

"The day before he died," I said, "he deposited five hundred dollars in his checking account. You know anything about that?"

"How would I know anything about it? No."

"He also wrote a check for the same amount to an unspecified payee. Wouldn't have been you, would it?"

"Why would he be writing me a five-hundred-dollar check?"

"Payback of a loan, maybe. I'm asking *you*."

"No. He didn't send me any check."

"So why no messages after Friday night? You quit on him, Barney?"

He didn't like that, which probably meant it was true. He drew himself up and slammed his hand down on the desk blotter. "I was busy over the weekend, I had other commitments—"

"Me, too, only mine were up in Creekside."

That bought me a glower. His lips formed an obscenity but he didn't give voice to it.

I said, "Exactly why do you think Eb tried to get in touch with me?"

"Pretty obvious, isn't it?"

"Say it anyway."

"He was having second thoughts. Wanted you to talk him out of killing himself."

"Did he? I thought so, too, for a while, but now I'm not so sure. Why me and not you? You're the one who was still his pal."

"But I'm not a hand-holder or a bleeding heart. You are."

"So he turned to me just like that, after four years? Not Bobbie Jean, not Joe, not a suicide hotline—me, the ex-partner he hated and wanted nothing to do with."

"Maybe he didn't hate you as much as you think. Maybe he was just ripped up by all the crap you laid on him before the split."

"He say that to you?"

"He didn't have to."

"Rivera the Omniscient. Did he mention my name either of the last two times you talked to him? Drunk or sober?"

"No, but that doesn't mean you weren't on his mind."

Anything was possible with a man in the throes of a suicidal depression. Including a visit to a breed of doctor he'd always distrusted. I asked Rivera, "Did he mention a psychologist named Richard Disney?"

". . . No. Why?"

"How about a Dr. Caslon? Night ER resident at S.F. General."

"No. What do they have to do with Eberhardt?"

"That's what I'd like to know," I said. "He made an appointment to see Disney last Tuesday. He didn't keep it—canceled at the last minute. Dr. Caslon is the one who referred him."

"An ER resident? What's the connection?"

"You tell me. Eberhardt say anything about a recent visit to the hospital?"

"No."

"Involvement in an accident of some kind?"

"No. Drunk and banged up his car, maybe."

"There wasn't any damage to his car."

"Fell down, got in a fight, whatever."

"Not according to Bobbie Jean."

"All right, so he met this Caslon some other way. On one of his cases. Or in a damn bar." Another peppermint disappeared between the chubby lips. "Why does it matter to you? What he did or didn't do at the end?"

"It doesn't matter to you?"

"No."

"Except where I'm concerned."

He sucked and chewed and said nothing.

"Well, maybe you don't care what triggered his suicide," I said, "but I do. Something had to push him over the edge. I want to know what it was."

"Maybe it was you," Rivera said.

". . . What?"

"His last resort, last hope, and you didn't care enough to call him back. *You* could've been the push."

The skin on my neck and between my shoulder blades seemed to bunch and curl upward. The possibility had never even occurred to me. I said, "Bullshit," but the denial lacked conviction in my own ears.

Me? For God's sake, me?

I ate an early dinner, food out of cans that I didn't really want, alone in my flat. Then I drove to San Francisco General, timing it so I arrived at the emergency room a little before seven o'clock. The time to catch Dr. Caslon, if I could catch him at all, was before he got swept up in ER's nightly parade of drug overdoses, accident trauma cases, shootings, stabbings, bludgeonings, and other instances of human suffering and human viciousness.

I'd been in the big beige-walled, linoleum-floored waiting room more times than I cared to remember, the last one less than a year ago to deliver a beating victim for treatment. On that night, ER had been experiencing one of its rare lulls; tonight, the staff was busy enough, though it was too early for the heaviest carnage—that usually comes somewhere around the witching hour—and a weeknight besides. A weeping woman cradling an arm swathed in a bloody towel was perched on one bench; on another, an Asian man whose face was a bas-relief of bruises and contusions was being comforted by members of his family; and on a gurney, awaiting transport into one of the examining rooms, lay a black kid about fifteen, his head wrapped in makeshift bandages. Not much business at all, really, for another evening in the urban jungle.

The admissions nurse, closeted behind heavy glass, listened to me tell her why I was there with an air of impassive and remote civility, as if there were several more layers of invisible glass between her world and mine; she'd seen and heard it all, and as long as she was here in this place, she wasn't letting any of it touch her up close and personal. She would have Dr. Caslon paged, she said, please sit down. I sat down. The page went out over the loudspeaker. I kept on sitting there while the weeping woman was ushered inside by a nurse and an attendant in crisp whites came out and wheeled the black kid away. Nobody paid any attention to the Asian man; he kept sitting there, too, in the bosom of his family, wearing a stunned expression under his mask of lumps.

At the end of ten minutes I went back to the admissions nurse to request another page. No sooner was the doctor's name out of my mouth than a voice behind me said, "I'm Dr. Caslon. What can I do for you?"

He was an African-American about thirty-five, with one of those rugged faces into which deep lines had already been cut, as if with an etching tool. By the time he was sixty he would resemble one of the Mt. Rushmore heads come to life and sculpted in black granite. Sooner than that, if he kept on working night shift in ER.

I introduced myself and showed him the photostat of my license. Nothing changed in his expression, then or when I said, "I'm here about a man named Eberhardt, Doctor. A former police lieutenant who committed suicide ten days ago."

"Yes?" he said, but not as if the name or the case meant anything to him.

"It's possible he was a patient here within the last two or three weeks. And that you may have been the attending physician."

"I don't recall the name. What sort of medical emergency?"

"I'm not sure there was one. Probably alcohol-related, if so."

"Half the cases we get are alcohol-related," Caslon said. "How did you get my name?"

"You referred him to a psychologist named Richard Disney."

"Did I? Well, Dr. Disney is an old friend of my father's; I often refer patients to him . . . Eberhardt, you said? Two to three weeks ago?"

"Yes."

Dr. Caslon did some cudgeling of his memory. No good; he shook his head.

"Maybe if I described him . . ."

Another headshake. "I see so many people," he said, and the smile that flashed on and off before he spoke again was bitterly humorless. "I remember wounds more easily than I remember faces."

"I understand, but this is important to me, Doctor. Could you check the admission records? I know that's an imposition, but all I want to know is whether or not Eberhardt was admitted, and if he was, when and why."

He glanced at his watch. "I don't have much time . . ."

"Please, Doctor."

"This man Eberhardt. A close friend of yours?"

"And my former partner. The suicide note he left is vague and there are so many unanswered questions . . ."

Caslon was young enough and compassionate enough to still be swayed by that kind of plea. He consulted his watch again and then said, "All right, but we'll have to make it quick. How do you spell the name?"

I told him. He stepped around me to the window, asked the nurse to check the files.

And thirty seconds later she said, "We have no admission record for anyone named Eberhardt, Doctor."

Caslon turned to me. "I'm sorry," he said, spreading his hands palms up.

"But you did refer him to Dr. Disney; Disney's receptionist was certain of it. How can that be, if he wasn't a patient of yours?"

"He may have gotten my name somehow and used it without my knowledge. A referral doesn't always come directly from one doctor to another, you know."

"You mean Eberhardt could've called Disney's office and used your name and they wouldn't have checked with you?"

"That's right. No reason for them to, unless the patient were to give them cause." Caslon's eyes shifted once more to his watch. "I'm sorry," he said again, distractedly this time, and started to move away.

I went after him, pressed one of my business cards into his hand and asked him to please give Eberhardt's name some more thought when he had free time. He looked at the card blankly, as if it were an unidentifiable object; tucked it into the pocket of his uniform jacket just as the entrance doors thumped open and a team of paramedics wheeled a stretcher inside. An old woman lay on the gurney, an oxygen mask fitted over her nose and mouth. In half a dozen strides Dr. Caslon was beside her, bending and talking to one of the paramedics; he'd forgotten all about me as soon as he saw his first patient of the night.

I'll never hear from him, I thought.

This finishes it. Now I'll never know.

13

It was frustration more than anything else that sent me over to the Portola district rather than home to my flat or Kerry's condo. Proximity had something to do with it, too—Silliman Street, just north of McLaren Park, is only a few miles from S. F. General and easily reachable by freeway—but I might have gone there even if it had been twenty miles out of the way. *Now I'll never know* kept repeating inside my head, a kind of mantra of the perverse. I could not make myself believe it because I didn't want to believe it; you can deny anything, even the most fundamental truths, if your desire for the opposite is strong enough.

That part of the city is working-class residential, on the downscale side as the result of any number of urban problems, one of them being the drug-infested housing projects on the Visitacion Valley side of McLaren Park. Dowdy row houses dominated the block between Gambier and Harvard; the one owned or rented by Danny Forbes was near the Gambier corner, small and saggy and nondescript. The double garage door under its bay windows was wide open, light from inside spilling out into the street. No other lights showed at the front.

Well, I thought, at least he's home. I had no idea what I would say to him. Scratch his surfaces, see if there was anything underneath worth burrowing after.

I parked across the street and went to the open door. A beat-up Mercury sedan, twelve to fifteen years old, squatted in one half of the cavelike interior. The other half was either a catchall area for garage-sale junk or a haphazard retreat created by a man who preferred holing up in his garage to occupying his normal living space. Among other items were a couch covered in hideous pseudo-leopard skin, a recliner with a busted footrest, an ancient six-sided poker table with a torn felt top, and a portable TV on a wobbly-looking stand. The TV was turned on; figures that looked as though they were trying to swim through snow made semiarticulate sounds punctuated by gunfire. Nobody was watching them or listening to the noise. For all I could see, the garage was empty.

I stepped inside by three paces for a better look. Next to the chair, I noticed then, was a low table on top of which sat an unopened bottle of Jack Daniel's and two glasses. I was staring at the bottle when wood creaked under descending footsteps and a voice said, "That you, Bert?" and then, explosively, "Hey! The hell *you* want?"

The stairs were at the rear, beyond the Merc; he came running off the last of the risers, around the front of the car and over to where I stood. Danny Forbes, dressed in a loud plaid sport jacket several years out of fashion and a pair of chocolate-colored slacks. His red hair had been slicked down with a gel whose sweetness assaulted my nostrils as he came up close. His broken nose had healed except for a knot at the bridge and what would probably be a permanent ten-degree list to the left; a scab showed where he'd been cut over one brow. His eyes snapped at me. So did his mouth.

"I don't know you, man. What the hell's the idea comin' in my garage?"

"Door's wide open. Lights and TV are on."

"That don't give you no right to walk in. Who are you? What you want?"

"Few minutes of your time."

"Whatever you're selling this time of night, I'm not interested."

"I'm not selling anything. I'm buying."

"Yeah? Buying what?" He licked thin lips; his eyes shifted, shifted back to hold on mine again. "I got nothing for sale."

"How about some information on a dead man named Eberhardt?"

He was the type who couldn't stand still. He'd been shuffling and bouncing around like one of those mean and hyperactive little dogs, but when I mentioned Eberhardt's name he froze. Not for long, but long enough. He backed up a step, trying not to look worried, and put another sheen of spit on his lips before he spoke again.

"Who the fuck's Eberhardt?"

"You know who he was, Danny. Man who killed himself on Bolt Street last week. The detective T. K. hired to find out who's been stealing from him and Nick."

"What's that got to do with me? I don't know nothing about any of that." He was dancing again. The eyes flicked to the watch on his wrist, flicked back to my face. "What're you, another one? T. K. hire you, too?"

"Suppose he did?"

"Suppose you get outta my garage before I throw you out."

"Something to hide, Danny?"

"Don't call me Danny. Only my friends call me Danny. I'm telling you, man, get out right now." Happy feet, and those shifty, shifty eyes. "I mean it."

"Sure thing, Danny. I'll be seeing you."

"Not if I see you first."

I took my time turning and walking out. He followed me onto the sidewalk, dancing and glaring, and stayed put as I crossed to the car and put myself inside. He was still there, still watching, as I drove off.

I followed Silliman as far as Yale, turned right, turned right again on Felton and came back to Gambier. Halfway along Gambier I shut off my lights and drifted slow toward the Silliman intersection. When I got to where I could see Forbes's house he was no longer standing in the outspill of light from the garage. Back inside somewhere; about all that was visible from this point was the back half of the Merc.

The last space at the corner was a No Parking zone. I eased the car into it and shut off the engine and sat hunched low in the dark to wait and watch.

It didn't take long, only about ten minutes. The fifth set of headlights that passed by on Silliman swung into Forbes's driveway and immediately went dark. The vehicle was a four-by-four of some kind; the light wasn't bright enough for me to tell the make or model. The man who got out and entered the garage was nobody I'd ever seen before—fat, bald, middle-aged, outfitted in a long leather coat over a pair of baggy pants held up by suspenders.

He could've been an old pal dropping by for a drink, but

I didn't think so. Forbes's eagerness to get rid of me said it was something else; so did the fact that he'd spiffed himself up, not so much in the fashion of a man preparing to socialize as of a salesman looking to impress a customer. I wasn't selling anything tonight, but maybe Danny Forbes was. Maybe I'd stumbled smack into a telltale piece of bad action.

Either way, the bottle of sour mash and the two glasses said they'd have at least one drink together. So I left the car quickly and hurried across Silliman and hugged shadows until I was close enough to the four-by-four to see that it was a Ford Bronco and to read the license plate. Then I hurried back to the car to write down the number and do some more waiting.

It was another ten minutes before they showed, both of them together. Forbes shut offf the lights and lowered the garage door, and they got into the Bronco. If they ended up in a bar or nightclub or bowling alley, I'd have to retrench. But the tingly fleeing in my gut said I hadn't misread either Danny Forbes or the situation.

I let the Bronco get under way to the east before I started the car; let it make a left-hand turn onto Harvard before I swung out after them. Highway 280 was where they were headed. They took the closest southbound entrance, and after that the tail was easy enough. A moderate flow of traffic helped, too. South to the Daly City exit, west on Highway 1 to Skyline Boulevard, south on Skyline to Westridge, right on Westridge to South Mayfair—and straight into the entrance drive of Mayfair Self-Storage. I rolled on past as the four-by-four stopped at the gate, traveled another block and turned around. They were inside, the gate closing behind them, as I passed the second time.

No point in trying to get in there or in waiting around here. I headed back to 280, back to the city and Silliman Street.

On the way I called directory assistance. Luck was still with me: there was a San Francisco listing for T. K. O'Hanlon, and the woman who answered my ring said he was in. His surprise gave way to happy rumblings when I told him why I was calling.

"I'm pretty sure Forbes is your thief," I said. "I just followed him and another guy to Mayfair Self-Storage in Daly City. I could be wrong about this, but I think the other man is a potential buyer and the stolen liquor is stored in one of the Mayfair units."

O'Hanlon said he'd be a son-of-a-bitch. "You won't let me hire you, then you go and nail the bastard on your own. I don't get it. How come?"

"I wasn't trying to nail him. Just happened to pick the right time to go talk to him."

"They still at this Mayfair Self-Storage, Forbes and the other guy?"

"Yeah, but I don't know for how long. It may be an outright buy tonight, but if so I doubt it'll be for every case he has stored. A better guess is that Forbes is showing off the contraband, negotiating a price for later pickup. The two of them went in the other one's four-by-four from Forbes's house, which means a return trip. Odds are they'd've taken two cars if more than a few cases were being sold and moved out tonight."

"I'll get hold of Nick," O'Hanlon said. "We'll meet you there in half an hour—"

"Too late by then. I've got a better idea."

"The cops?"

"No, not yet. Not enough proof to bring in the law. I could

be wrong—I wasn't able to get inside the storage facility to verify that the liquor is there—and we don't want to run the risk of a lawsuit."

"So what's your idea?"

"You and your brother meet me at Forbes's house. It's on Silliman Street off Highway 280, Portola district. Either we wait there for Forbes, or if he's already back when you get there, we go right in and brace him. If he is dirty, that should crack him."

"Sounds good to me."

"Two conditions, T. K. No rough stuff unless Forbes or the other man provokes it. And I get at least ten minutes alone with Forbes at the outset."

"How come you and him alone?"

"Personal reasons. Fair enough?"

"Fair enough," he agreed.

"You or your brother have a cell phone or car phone?"

"I got a cell phone I can bring along."

"Okay. I'll be at Forbes's house long before you; I'm almost back there now. When you get off the freeway and into his neighborhood, call me and I'll tell you where I am and what the situation is and we'll take it from there."

He agreed to that, too, and I told him my number and the location of Forbes's house. He said then, "We owe you, pal, and the O'Hanlons always pay their debts. I'm not talking handshake, either."

"The handshake's enough. I don't want your money, T. K. All I want are those ten minutes with Forbes."

"You think he had something to do with Eberhardt killing himself? That it?"

"Could be," I said. "One way or another I'm going to find out."

* * *

I'd been parked for twenty minutes in the same place as before, in the No Parking zone on the corner of Gambier and Silliman, when the Ford Bronco showed up. Trip to look over the merchandise and negotiate a price, and maybe a small sale and pickup; there hadn't been time for anything else. The four-by-four stood idling in front of Forbes's house, its headlights blazing, for less than a minute. Then Forbes got out alone and the bald guy drove off.

I was tempted to go over there and brace Forbes then and there, get it done with. But I'd committed myself to O'Hanlon, and besides, the three of us—three big, hard guys—ganging up on the little bugger was bound to rattle him more than just me going at him alone. I stayed put, watched him unlock the garage door and disappear inside. A couple of minutes later, a light behind drawn blinds showed in one of the upstairs windows.

Another ten minutes, and the mobile phone buzzed. The O'Hanlons were a few blocks away. I told T. K. where I was and pretty soon a white Cadillac Eldorado turned off Silliman, drifted past me and to the curb at the first available space. I got out and went up to meet them where the three of us couldn't be seen from Forbes's house.

Nick O'Hanlon was several years younger than his brother, built along the same blocky lines and even bigger—six three and a solid two hundred and fifty pounds. He let T. K. do the talking. A man that large doesn't need words to make his presence felt.

T. K. asked, "Both of 'em at the house?"

"Just Forbes."

"Too bad."

"If the other one did make a buy tonight, he won't get away with anything. I've got his license number." I passed over the sheet of paper from my notebook. "One question before we go over there, T. K."

"Sure, go ahead."

"You told me five cases of Glenlivet and two of sour mash disappeared weekend before last. What brand of sour mash?"

"Jack Daniel's."

"Yeah, I thought so." I took a couple of breaths to ease the tightness in my chest. "Okay, let's do it."

We trooped over there and up the front stairs, each of us walking quiet. I leaned on the doorbell. Ten seconds passed, and I leaned some more, and then Forbes's voice came warily from inside, "Hey, lay off. Who is it?"

I nudged T. K. He said, "T. K. O'Hanlon. Need to talk to you, Danny boy. Open up."

Forbes stalled for a little time, but he didn't have much choice other than trying to run out the back way. He opted for a lame bluff instead; unlocked and opened the door wearing a puzzled smile. "Hey, T. K., what—" The rest of it got swallowed and the smile turned upside down when he saw the three of us standing there. His hand twitched on the inner knob, as if the thought of jamming the door shut had crossed his mind. But Nick O'Hanlon already had a shoulder against it and was crowding inside. T. K. and I followed, forcing Forbes back into a cluttered and sparsely furnished front parlor.

"What's the idea?" he said. "What's going on?"

"You know what's going on, you little piece of shit," T. K. said. "So do we now. You're the one's been stealing from us."

"That's a goddamn lie—"

I said, "Mayfair Self-Storage in Daly City."

"I don't know what you're talkin' about," he said, but some of the bluster and most of the toughness were leaking out of him. He began to twitch and dance the way he had in the garage earlier. "Listen—"

"Shut up," T. K. said. He looked at me. "Ten minutes alone with him, right?"

"It may take longer."

"Take as much time as you need."

I said to Forbes, "What's through that door over there?"

"Screw you. I don't hafta stand for this—"

"That's right. You can sit for it. Nick, you want to help me settle him down?"

Nick said, "Pleasure," and we each took a piece of Forbes and half carried him through the doorway into a dirty kitchen and banged him onto a dinette chair. Then Nick went out, wordlessly, and left him to me.

"We're going to talk about Eberhardt," I said. "You and me, Forbes, until you tell me everything I want to know."

No answer. He sat there trying to reestablish his belligerent attitude and not making much headway.

"He caught you, didn't he? Saturday or Sunday night, red-handed."

His eyes shifted, his body twitched. "I don't know what you're talkin' about."

"He was staked out in the alley and you didn't know it until it was too late. You got into the warehouse, came out with the liquor, and he grabbed you. How much of the sour mash did you give him?"

"I don't know what you're talkin' about."

"He drank cheap whiskey—Four Roses. It was all he could afford. But he had a bottle of Jack Daniel's the night he died. He had to've gotten it from you."

Fidgets and glowers.

"Come on, Forbes. You want this to go on all night? Or how about if I call the O'Hanlons in here and let them beat it out of you? I'll do that if you don't start talking. Believe it."

He believed it. The last of his toughness dribbled out of him like sand from a ruptured sack. His shoulders slumped; the sinewy body went slack. Only his hands continued to move, lifting, falling, bumping into each other in midair as if he no longer had any control over them."

"All right," he muttered. "The fuck's the use now? Yeah, he caught me. Sunday night. Yeah."

"And you put up a fight. That's how you got the busted nose and the eye cut. Eberhardt."

"Old bastard like him, and half drunk." Sullen now, expression and voice both. "Dark on the loading dock. Otherwise it'd've been his ass that got kicked."

"Sure it would. Staggering drunk he was twice as tough as you think you are. How much Jack Daniel's did he take?"

"Two lousy bottles. That's all he wanted."

"No it isn't. He wanted money, too. Five hundred dollars."

"Yeah."

"Five hundred not to haul your sorry butt to the police. Five hundred to keep his mouth shut and let you leave with the cases of whiskey." The words were like fecal matter on my tongue; I spat them out.

"Yeah," Forbes said. "Yeah, five hundred. I only had fifty on me. He took that, told me I'd better have the rest in cash next day. I had it."

"When'd you pay him off?"

"Monday night, like he wanted."

"Where?"

"Bolt Street, where else?" he said, and added bitterly, "I wasn't the only one ripping off the O'Hanlons."

"You figured he'd be there Tuesday night, too, so you went back and snuck up on him and shot him."

Forbes jerked upright, came halfway out of his chair; I pushed him back down. For the first time real fear showed in his shifty eyes. "No! Jesus, I didn't go near him again after Monday, I swear it. Why would I kill him?"

"So you wouldn't have to pay any more blackmail."

"No, he said the five hundred was a one-time thing—"

"Every blackmailer says that and you know it."

"Jesus, listen . . . if I wanted to kill him, why wouldn't I do it Monday night? Huh? Why would I pay him the five hundred and then go back the next night and shoot him?"

"You tell me."

"I didn't! I was with a woman Tuesday night, all night at her place, I told the cops that. Give you her name, you go talk to her, she'll tell you. I stole the liquor, okay, I admit it, but I'm not a killer, man."

I stared holes through him.

"You gotta believe me," he said, whining now. "He shot himself, he musta. I heard about it, I couldn't believe he'd do something like that right after I paid him the five hundred. It didn't make no sense to me, but I was glad about it, sure, I figured I was off the hook . . ."

Babbling now, and I couldn't stand to listen to any more. He was telling the truth; he hadn't killed Eberhardt. Eberhardt had shot himself. I told him to shut up, reached down and yanked him out of the chair.

"Now you listen and listen good. You say you didn't shoot Eberhardt, I'll give you the benefit of the doubt. But you keep your mouth shut about him when the cops question you again. Don't tell them he caught you, don't tell them he smacked you around, don't tell them about the two bottles of Jack or the five hundred, don't even mention his name. You understand me, Forbes? None of that happened."

"Yeah, yeah, I understand. I won't say nothing, I swear to God I won't."

"Better not, because Eberhardt was once a cop and if the police have any reason to suspect you might've killed him . . ."

I didn't need to finish it; his eyes said he'd gotten the message. Enough, I thought. I pushed him to the door, out into the front room.

"I'm finished with him," I said to the O'Hanlons. "He's all yours."

Nick O'Hanlon came over and caught hold of Forbes's arm. The look on his face was that of a hound taking possession of a hunk of raw meat.

I motioned to T. K. and he went to the front door with me. "One favor, T. K.," I said.

"Sure. Name it."

"When you get around to having Forbes arrested, I don't want any of the credit. You and Nick were suspicious of him, you're the ones who followed him to Daly City. Leave me out of it entirely."

"If that's the way you want it."

"Not much of this is the way I want it," I said. "Most of it is just plain lousy."

He didn't know what I was talking about. And just as well he didn't ask because I was through with him, too, for tonight and for good.

14

So Eberhardt had been much dirtier than I'd imagined. Corrupt his whole life, maybe, down deep at the core; sure as hell rotten at the end. My partner the crook. My pal the stranger. Shaking down a two-bit thief for five hundred dollars and a couple of bottles of Jack Daniel's. So far gone, so lost, that even his final act of corruption had been weak, petty.

Was that the trigger, then? Disgust, self-loathing at how low he'd sunk?

Part of it, possibly—but there had to be more, some other factor. Who had been the recipient of that five-hundred-dollar check? And what was it in payment for? Key questions that still had no answers. I'd know the answers when the check finally cleared, unless for some reason it wasn't cashed at all; but even if I knew that much, I might never get at the whole truth. Right now, with the foul taste of Eberhardt's dishonesty in my mouth, the prospect didn't bother me as much as it had before. I was no longer sure I cared to find out any more than I already had.

I went to my flat because I needed to be alone tonight. Too late to call Kerry; it was nearly eleven-thirty. But she'd understand when I explained it all to her. Our marriage worked because we were sensitive to each other's needs: when one of us had to have space, the space was allowed without fuss or question. There for each other even when we weren't together, in spirit and by tacit agreement.

I rummaged around in the fridge, found a can of Bud Light. It did nothing for the sour taste; in fact the smell and the first sip built a faint nausea that spread upward into my throat. I poured the beer into the sink, returned to the living room and put all the lights on and some moody jazz on my old turntable. Then, in spite of what I'd been thinking in the car, in spite of myself, I sat at the desk and went through Eberhardt's papers again item by item.

Waste of time, just jerking myself around. It was all dead matter in every sense of the term. And yet when I was done, an hour or so later, I had the feeling I'd missed something, that something important had been staring me in the face twice now and I'd overlooked it both times. It was like smoke in my mind; I'd reach for it, almost grasp it, and it would break up, drift away.

Bed. But no sleep. And lying there, I wondered if I had after all been jerking my own chain; if the smoke was imaginary, just one more illusion among the many . . .

Dark place, narrow and chill, sometimes moving and sometimes stationary, an alley or tunnel or train whispering through a tunnel, and I was running walking stumbling toward a dot or spot of white, yellow, white glow, light glow, growing larger and then smaller and then it winked out and

I was in clinging satin blackness and somewhere a voice said, "Join me for a midnight snack?" and all at once I was frightened and I tried to stop turn around run away but the walls bound in closer and the train whispered faster and the voice said, "Corner ahead, just come around the corner," and I ran walked ran and the corner was there, I felt it with my hands, cold cold cold as death, and dragged myself around it and a door loomed up huge and I caught its handle and yanked the door open and I was in a car, sliding into a car, and Eberhardt was sitting behind the wheel with the Magnum in his mouth like an obscene lollipop and he mumbled something around the muzzle, "Quit looking for Trigger buddy boy Roy Rogers already had him stuffed," and then he laughed and laughed, a madman's laugh, and I yelled No! and he said, "Let's eat" and the gun went off with a deafening roar but the hole and the blood appeared in his chest not his head and his blood spattered on me on me all over me . . .

I was awake for good or bad at five-thirty, up by six, climbing the walls by seven-fifteen, out of there and down to O'Farrell and into the office before eight. Cinder-eyed and headachey from lack of sleep, the remnants of the nightmare still adhering like dirty strands of spider silk to the corners of my mind. I made coffee, sloshed three cups on top of the two I'd had at the flat. All the caffeine worsened the headache, darkened my mood even more.

Tamara showed up promptly at nine, too cheerful and with a mischievous glint in her eyes. The glint faded some when she got a good look at me. "All beat up again," she said. "Something happen last night?"

"Nothing for you to worry about."

"Walks like a man, growls like a bear." She hung up her

coat, and when I glanced at her again she was standing midway between her desk and mine, grinning at me. "Never guess where me and Horace be going on Saturday."

"Horace and I," I said automatically. "Are going."

"Not in my hizzy, man. You never heard of Ebonics?"

"I'm not in the mood for Ebonics. Or guessing games."

She didn't argue; she was leading up to something else. "We're going out to Concord," she said. "Horace's brother's part owner of a kennel out there. I ever tell you that?"

"Not that I remember."

"Yeah. Zeke and his partner raise purebred Lhasa apsos, mostly sell 'em to dog-show people. You know what I'm saying? So some males they keep for stud, but one had a problem and they had to have him fixed. Mr. Mighty."

"Stupid name for a dog."

"Bitches didn't think so," she said. "So anyway, on Saturday we be hangin' with Zeke while Mr. Mighty gets him a brand-new set of balls."

My reaction to that—a blank stare—disappointed her. So did my verbal response. "Is that some kind of joke?"

"No joke," she said. "Polypropylene."

"What?"

"That's what they're made of. Polypropylene."

"Tamara, what the hell're you talking about?"

"Balls," she said. "See, it's this new process vets have for neutered male dogs, give 'em imitation balls that look and feel like the real thing. Supposed to build up their confidence. The dogs and their owners, not the vets."

"Come on," I said.

"No lie. It's called CTI."

"Which stands for what?"

"Canine Testicular Implants. Neuticles."

I didn't say anything.

"That's what they're called. Also the name of the company that makes 'em."

I didn't say anything.

"I knew you wouldn't believe it. I didn't believe it either, first time I heard about it." She fished a sheet of paper out of the huge raggedy purse she carries and plopped it in front of me. "Look at this flyer."

I looked. Neuticles. CTI—Canine Testicular Implant. Replicates the canine testicle in size, shape, and weight. Lets any-size dog look and feel the same as it did before neutering.

"How do they know, huh?" Tamara said.

"How do they know what?"

"That the new balls feel the same to the dog? Zeke says Neuticles feel the same to a human—you know, when you poke or squeeze one."

"Tamara."

"Hey, that's what Zeke says. Show-dog owners always doing stuff like that. At one show Horace went to with Zeke, the owner of a puli . . . You know what a puli is? No? Hungarian sheep-herding dog, long ropy black hair. Anyway, one of this puli's testicles got drawn up inside because the dog was nervous or something and there's a rule that male show dogs not only can't be neutered but have to have *both* their balls, so when the judge could only find one and was gonna disqualify the dog, the owner—"

"Tamara."

"—the owner reached up and felt around and found the missing ball and yanked it—"

"Tamara!"

"Well, Horace swears it's true and he don't lie."

"Go to work," I said.

"Polypropylene testicles for dogs. Man. What'll they think of next, huh? I'd still like to know—"

"For Christ's sake stop babbling and do your job."

The words sounded as harsh to me as they must have to Tamara. Both her grin and her good humor died; anger flared in the brown eyes, tightened the edges of her mouth. For a few seconds I thought she would snap back at me in kind. But the anger died, too, and some of the old, hard cynicism reshaped her expression.

"Yassuh, boss. 'Scuse me, boss."

"Tamara . . ."

"Serious work bein' done 'round here. Ain't no time for jokin' and laughin'." Then she dropped the dialect and said in her normal voice, "Balls." She stalked to her desk and banged her purse on the floor, her behind down on the chair, and made more noise than was necessary hooking up her PowerBook.

I wanted to apologize to her but I had no words. The only ones in my head were a paraphrase of what she'd said a minute ago: *What'll we find out next?* The question and the memory it'd triggered: Eberhardt and me, right here in this room, a year or two before the bust-up. Bobbie Jean had found an article in some magazine, called "You Broke Your *What?*" and documenting a number of actual cases of human penile fracture. Neither of us had ever heard of this phenomenon, and it had led to some speculation of one kind and another, and I'd made a joke out of the idea of a man having his broken member in a cast, all his friends coming around to sign it. But Eberhardt hadn't seen the humor. Dead serious issue to him. *How would you like it if it happened to you, wise guy?* Serious work bein' done 'round here. Ain't no time for jokin' and laughin'.

Damn! Everything reminded me of him lately, everything I did seemed to be colored by my relationship with him and my reaction to his descent into suicide. Beating myself up with all the memories large and small, taking out my frustrations on others like Tamara who didn't deserve such shabby treatment. The problem was mine, mine and Eberhardt's. The two of us wrapped up so tightly together that it was no longer easy to establish separation or perspective. Too often I looked at him and saw myself. And when you look at yourself in the reflected light of truth and insight, sometimes you don't like what you see. Don't like yourself much at all. And you begin to realize that there is sham and fantasy in your self-perceptions too . . .

I tried to make myself concentrate on preliminary work on the suspicious accident-insurance claim. No good. I thought about calling Bobbie Jean again, but I didn't do it. It would be cruel to keep bugging her the way I was bugging myself. She'd told me she would talk to the bank again about the five-hundred-dollar check; if and when it was cashed, I'd hear from her.

Another few minutes crawled away to the accompaniment of machine noise—the PowerBook's peckety keyboard and then the rattle and clatter of the printer. For Christ's sake, I thought, why keep on sitting here like this, letting a wall build for no good reason? Your fault; make it right. I stood and went to Tamara's desk. She didn't look up, so I cleared my throat. She still didn't look up.

"Tamara, I'm sorry. I had no cause to take out my crappy mood on you. It won't happen again . . ."

She wasn't listening. Not because she was still peeved, I thought, but because she was staring at what was coming out of the printer. The thing quit clattering and she reached over, tore off the sheet. "Yeah, interesting," she said, and wheeled around and cocked an eye at me. The eye was free of both cynicism and anger; either she'd forgotten I'd snapped at her or had heard my apology and decided to accept it without comment. Letting me off easy.

"What's interesting?"

"News story I just downloaded from the Santa Rosa paper."

"Something to do with the Arco skip-trace?"

"No. I finished that last night. Erskine case. All the stuff you told me kept dancing around in my head, so I figured I'd do some cruising on the information highway, see could I pull up anything new."

I said, "No point in it, with the client dead."

"So now I'm the only one with doubts about how he got that way?"

"Okay. What'd you find out?"

"Nothing much about Erskine, or Nelson or Woolfox. But Gail Kendall . . . here, take a look."

I read through the printout. The news story was nine years old and had made the front page of the Santa Rosa *Press-Democrat*. An out-of-work architect with a history of domestic violence, one Eugene Finley, had gone on an early-morning shooting rampage in Glen Ellen, wounding one of his neighbors and killing another's dog with a shotgun; then he'd taken his wife captive and barricaded the two of them inside their house, threatening to kill her and then himself. The local police had called in the county SWAT team and hostage negotiator, and after a five-hour standoff Finley had agreed to give himself up. He'd released his wife, but as soon as she was out the front door he'd come into the doorway with the shotgun and tried to blow her head off. He'd missed, but one of the SWAT marksmen hadn't; Finley had died instantly with a bullet in his brain. The wife who had narrowly escaped harm was Gail Kendall Finley, "a noted Sonoma Valley wine chemist."

Tamara said when I was done reading, "No surprise Nelson and Kendall got to be friends. Went through the same kind of shit, had their scars in common. Sisters."

"But not necessarily partners in crime."

"Makes a big coincidence even bigger, though, right? Erskine shows up after four years and a few days later he's dead meat. And now we find out the ex and her best bud are battered women and Kendall's old man died from lead in the head, even if it was a SWAT cop who put it there."

"It's still circumstantial," I said. "No proof of a connection or any kind of collusion."

"So there isn't one? You believe that?"

"I don't know what I believe anymore."

"*Feels* like murder, doesn't it? Feels that way to me."

"Tamara, what it feels like to the two of us isn't relevent. There's nothing I could do even if I wanted to. It's a police matter, out of my hands."

"Didn't stop you some other times I know about."

"You know too much. I'm finished with the Erskine shooting and so are you from now on. Clear?"

Her mouth said, "You the boss man." Her too-wise smile said the only person I was fooling here was myself.

Another night alone in my flat. Another session with the paper remnants of Eberhardt's final months. And the same zero as last night, the numbers and words all blurring together into an unrecognizable mass like a stew cooked so long you couldn't tell one ingredient from another. Yet I had the same nagging feeling I was missing something—and the same worry that the feeling was imaginary. My subconscious playing games with me, creating shimmery apparitions and then daring me to catch one before it faded away?

Another night alone in bed, watching the dark, then entering the dark place . . .

. . . *narrow and chill, sometimes moving and sometimes stationary, an alley or tunnel or train whispering through a tunnel, running walking stumbling toward a dot or spot of white, yellow, white glow, light glow, growing larger and then smaller and then it winked out and I was in clinging satin blackness and somewhere a voice said, "Join me for a midnight snack?"* . . .

Cracking up a little.

That was how I felt in the morning, as if there were tiny fissures forming and spreading inside my head and if I didn't do something to stop the process, and soon, the fissures would deepen and widen and eventually split me into ragged eggshell halves. And what would pop out like a mutated baby chick was a core thing, a kind of capering and gibbering id that would run around in mad circles until it collapsed and died of sheer frustrated exhaustion. There was a horrifically funny edge to that, but I didn't laugh. This was not a good time to be treating anything lightly, least of all my own dark side.

What I needed to do, I thought as I showered, was to get my mind into something besides Eberhardt's life, Eberhardt's death. And keep it there until I regained some perspective. Another case, one that required physical as well as mental activity; I'd spent too much time sitting around the office lately. Fine, except that the only case I had working was the supermarket accident claim, and that was routine and would likely require a lengthy stakeout before I wrapped it up—the worst possible inactivity I could indulge in right now.

What else? Nothing else.

Just Ira Erskine.

No, I thought. I'd meant what I said to Tamara, never mind her too-wise smile. If a private investigator doesn't have a paying client, he can't legally conduct an investigation—and that goes double in a police matter involving a fatality. I'd be inviting any number of hassles if I tried to stick my nose into what would almost surely go down as an accidental shooting, even if it wasn't.

Airtight alibis and a man shot to death in a closed-up motel room . . . how *could* it be homicide? How and who? Tough nut, and plenty of activity needed in trying to crack it. Something to *do*, whether or not I got anywhere.

Mistake. Potentially a big one.

Sure.

Out of it and staying out.

Sure.

I thought I had myself convinced by the time I left the flat. Three and a half hours later I was on my way across the Golden Gate Bridge, headed for Sonoma County.

15

The Pinecrest Lodge was on the northern outskirts of Healdsburg, along a frontage road that paralleled Highway 101 and clearly visible from the freeway. Not large and not small—some sixty units in a pair of two-story wings that extended out from a central lobby, restaurant, and lounge. All the room entrances appeared to face the highway; close behind the complex were stands of trees and a couple of low hills that folded in against each other. On the thirty-foot-tall sign above the entrance drive, the word "Vacancy" burned palely in red neon.

The next exit was a short distance ahead; I took it and came back on the frontage road. This early on a Friday afternoon, only a few cars were parked in the lot. I added mine to the total and entered a lobby that looked and felt and smelled like every motel lobby from California to Maine; the only difference was that they had the heat turned up too high. Nothing at all special about the Pinecrest that I could see. Quite a comedown from the St. Francis for a man like

Erskine, but then he hadn't been interested in comfort or anything else except his ex-wife when he came up here from the city. He'd picked the motel for its location, no other reason. And it would've been his last stopping place, I thought, even if he hadn't died here. He'd been ready to die somewhere in Sonoma County, but not alone: I had little doubt that he would have killed Sondra Nelson and then himself if he'd had the chance.

Behind the desk, a young woman wearing a green blazer with a gold pocket crest of three pines was busy on both the phone and a computer keyboard. She and I were alone in the lobby. I smiled at her; she smiled back, miming the words "I'll be with you in a moment, sir." The other party kept her on the line longer than she anticipated, though. She raised her eyebrows and shook her head as if she were mildly exasperated, then smiled at me again. In response I told her silently that it was all right, I was in no hurry. So we had already established a rapport when the conversation finally ended.

"Sorry about that," she said as if she meant it. "Would you like a room, sir?"

"Well, I'm not sure." The apologetic note I squeezed into my voice sounded genuine enough. "You do have more than one vacancy?"

"Yes we do. Our rates—"

"Oh, the rate doesn't matter. What matters is the room."

"Sir?"

"Not to me, you understand. Any room is fine with me, all I care about is that it has a bed in it. But my wife . . . well, she's picky." I manufactured a sigh. "Very picky."

The young woman nodded and smiled and said, "Picky in what way?"

"The size of the room, for one thing. Do you have any suites or large rooms with fireplaces?"

"No, I'm sorry, we don't."

"So all of your accommodations are the same? I mean, I understand some rooms are singles and some doubles, but the size and general floor plan are identical in each?"

"That's right. A few do have connecting doors that you can leave open to make up a suite—"

"Not an option, I'm afraid. I wonder . . . I know this is an imposition, but would it be all right if I looked at one of your ground-floor rooms? My wife insists on the ground floor, and the size and layout really are very important to her."

"Well . . ."

"Just a brief look. I'm sure it'll be suitable, but if it isn't and I've already checked in . . . I'm being a pest, aren't I?"

"No, no, not at all. I'd take you out and show you one of the vacancies but I'm here alone right now . . . Would you mind if I gave you a key and let you go look by yourself?"

"That's very kind of you. Five minutes or so is all I need."

"Take as much time as you like, sir."

We traded smiles again, and I went on my way with a key. Simple as that. I hoped the next person who took advantage of the nice young woman's trust had motives as relatively benign as mine.

The number on the key was 116, a room more or less in the middle of the south wing. Average-size rectangle, only slightly deeper than it was wide, with a half wall separating the bed and sitting area from a bathroom cubicle and an adjoining space containing a countertop with two sinks, a mirror, and an open closet. Double bed, round table and two uncomfortable cane-backed chairs, dresser, writing desk, TV set on a stand. Blue-and-green decor, blue-and-green seascapes that nobody in his right mind would want to steal screwed tight to the walls. If the room were to survive intact into the twenty-second century, anthropologists of that time could stick it into a museum as a perfect example of Standard American Motel Room, Late Twentieth Century.

I stepped inside, leaving the door partway open, and took a long look at it, the jamb, and the locking mechanisms. The knob lock was a deadbolt and so was the security lock above it. There was also a chain fastener of the sort that makes some people feel safe in strange surroundings, as well as in their own home, but that in reality provides little protection; a hefty twelve-year-old can kick or shoulder through ninety-eight percent of them. The deadbolts were of decent manufacture and durable enough, and the door here fit snugly in the jamb, which indicated that the same would be true in the other units. Battle had told me both deadbolts had been set in Erskine's room; the chain lock must've been off for the cleaning woman to passkey her way in. There were methods an expert locksmith could use to gimmick a couple of deadbolts like these, but the average person working without foreknowledge and the proper tools couldn't hope to manage it. Besides, the cleaning woman and the two guests had been close enough to hear the shots and to get out to where they could see Erskine's door in a hurry. There would not have been time for anyone in the room to either gimmick the locks or get out through the door unseen.

The same went for the curtained window next to it. Two overlapping halves, one of which you could slide open to let in air; that half was screened. The latch was a simple snap type, but the sliding half was fitted with one of those security bolts that you can screw down to prevent the window from opening even when the latch is released. Forget this window as an exit, too.

That left the bathroom. It wasn't much larger than an upended packing crate, with just enough space for a toilet and a compact tub and shower; put three people in it and you'd be inviting an orgy. The only window in there was above the tub—an oblong, overlapping-halves job similar to the one out front, except that it was much smaller and the glass was opaque and unscreened. Three feet long, not much more than eighteen inches high. I swung over into the tub, leaned up to look more closely at the window. Same kind of snap catch as the other but without the screw-down bolt. I slid the one half open. No outside screen or bars. I stuck my head through the opening. Trees, hillsides, not much else to see.

Somebody *could* have gotten out this way without being seen, all right, but it would've had to have been a slender and agile somebody to squeeze through such a small opening. I couldn't have done it if my life depended on it. Gail Kendall couldn't have, and I doubted Woolfox would've fit, either. Sondra Nelson . . . maybe. But she was the one with the tightest alibi of all: jury duty fifteen miles away.

I took a couple more passes through the room, looking at each of its contents, trying to figure an angle. Suppose the shot the maid and guests heard wasn't the one that had killed Erskine? Some sort of second-shot delay gimmick, like putting a long, slow fuse on a stick of dynamite. Firecrackers, air-filled and then popped paper bags, a shot recorded on tape and played back later . . . I'd heard of or personally encountered all of those little tricks. The problem with something like that, though, was that the perp either had to be on the premises, which in this case wasn't feasible, or there had to be some leftover evidence to reveal the gaffe. Battle would've mentioned having found the remains of a blown firecracker or anything else that obviously didn't belong, and if there'd been a recording device he'd have replayed its tape; trained investigators don't miss things like that. And there was nothing in the room or its furnishings that suggested any cute possibilities. Scratch the second-shot delay theory.

What else? Some other type of misdirection? I couldn't imagine any that fit the circumstances as Battle had outlined them to me. If Erskine *had* been murdered, even with malice aforethought, it had to've been a simple, straightforward crime. Not enough time to plan anything elaborate or even clever; and homicides involving overheated passions don't generate fancy schemes anyway. Any trickery would've been improvised on the spot, to take advantage of the situation as it developed, and in this case it didn't seem likely or even possible. Scratch trickery of any kind. What you saw was all there was. So if it had been murder, the perp had gone out through that tiny bathroom window. Or managed to hide behind the door and then slip out after the cleaning woman and male guest came in—an even more unlikely prospect.

I left the room, locked the door behind me. As I started to turn back toward the lobby, I spied a maid's cart down at the end of the wing. Sight of it prodded me into a switch of direction. When I neared the cart, a middle-aged woman in uniform came out through the open door of room 130 with an armload of dirty linen. She looked to be Latina, and tired and beaten down by her daily grind. She gave me an indifferent look that didn't change much when I said, "Excuse me. I'd like to talk to you, please."

"Yes?"

"About what happened here last week. The shooting."

She rolled her eyes upward. Muttered to herself, *"Ai, Dios mio. Un otro agente inquiridor con otro interrogación. Cada vez más."*

"No tender nada un secreto, eh, señora?"

". . . Habla Español," she said, surprised.

"Sí, un poquito." She thought I was a cop, a mistake a lot of people make: I have the look and I walk the walk. I let her think it. You can't be accused of impersonating an *agente inquiridor* unless you make the claim yourself; other people's perceptions don't count. In English I asked, "Are you the woman who found the dead man?"

"No, that was Carmelita."

"Is she here now?"

"*Sí*. Upstairs."

"I'd appreciate it if you'd take me to her."

"Como quieras," she said and sighed, and led me up the nearest staircase to the second floor.

Carmelita was vacuuming one of the rooms back toward the front; she shut the machine off when we walked in. She was younger and thinner than my escort, but hard work and hard living had already carved the same deep lines of weariness in her brown face. Looking at the two of them put me in mind of the volatile rhetoric of too many compassionless politicians and their minions these days. Yes, sir, all those south-of-the-border immigrants, legals and illegals both, sure do have an easy time of it here in the land of plenty, stealing jobs and living the good life. Just ask them. Just spend five minutes looking at the world through their eyes.

The older woman spoke to the younger one in rapid Spanish, too fast and idiomatic for me to follow. Carmelita looked nervous and a little frightened. One kind of cynic might have said it was because she didn't have a green card and wanted nothing to do with authority in any form; my kind of cynic thought it was probably an ingrained fear born of poverty, oppression, and racial hatred.

Carmelita admitted in broken English that she had found "the dead one"—she crossed herself as she spoke the words—but had told the other *policía* all about it, she didn't know anything more, she was only a *mujer de la limpieza*, a cleaning woman. I asked her in Spanish to tell it one more time, *por favor*, but the politeness didn't do much to put her at ease. She rattled off her story, not making eye contact, getting it all out in a rush as if she were purging herself of a virulent form of bile.

Erskine had had the end room on the ground floor, north wing; she'd been two rooms away, waiting for "the Mr. and Mrs. Doyle" to move their luggage out so she could clean. All three had heard the report at seven-forty. She knew the time because Mr. Doyle had looked at his watch and later she'd heard him tell the police. Mrs. Doyle said the noise sounded like a gunshot; Mr. Doyle said it *was* a gunshot and ran to Erskine's room and listened at the door and then pounded on it. When no one answered, he told Carmelita she had better use her passkey, somebody might be hurt inside. She hadn't wanted to do that, it was against motel rules, but when he insisted she gave in. She and Mr. Doyle both went inside. "I wan to scream when I see the dead one," she said, and crossed herself again, "but I can't make a sound." Mr. Doyle took her arm, led her outside, told her to stay there with his wife while he went to the lobby to call the police. And that was all that had happened, all she knew.

I said, "Just a few questions, Carmelita. *Sí usted no tiene inconveniente*. How long was it from the time you heard the shot to the time you unlocked the door?"

"I doan know for sure. *Quatro, cinco minutos*."

Enough time for somebody to wiggle out through that narrow bathroom window; more than enough time. "When Mr. Doyle listened at the door, did he say if he heard anything inside?"

"No, he doan say."

"Did he act as if he had?"

Headshake.

"When you were inside the room, did you or Mr. Doyle go to look in the bathroom?"

"The bathroom? No, *señor*. We go out again, quick."

"How quick? *Un minuto? Dos?*"

"No! *Diez segundo, cuando más.*"

Ten seconds at the most. "Did you or Mr. Doyle touch anything in the room?"

"No. I wan to pick up the *pitillo* but he doan let me."

"What cigarette, Carmelita?"

"On the carpet. Mr. Doyle say doan touch nothing so the carpet, it gets burn."

"Where was it burning the carpet?"

"Where?" She shook her head, not understanding.

"Close to the dead man or not?"

"Close." Carmelita shivered. "Almost burn *him*, his hand."

"As if he'd dropped it when he fell."

"*Sí.*"

"And where was he lying, exactly?"

"Near the bed."

"Closer to the bed than the table?"

"*Sí.*"

"You're sure of that?"

"The bed, *sí.*"

"Where was the chair he'd been sitting in?"

"*Como?*"

"Was it on the floor too, knocked over?"

"No. At the table. Both chairs."

"Close to the table, you mean?"

"*Sí*, close."

"The things he was using to clean his gun—rags, oil, things like that. Were some of them on the floor?"

"I doan think so."

"All still on the table?"

"*Sí*."

"Knocked over, scattered around?"

Blank look, another headshake; she said something in Spanish to the older woman, who shrugged and remained silent. The older one didn't want any part of this interrogation.

I said patiently to Carmelita, "When you bump into a table, the things that are on it sometimes fall over, even if they don't roll off onto the floor. *Comprende?*"

"*Sí*."

"Is that the way the things on the table looked?"

"No, *señor*. Everything . . . you know, not fall over."

Battle hadn't mentioned the burning cigarette to me; or the positioning of the chairs and the body; or the fact that the cleaning supplies were still in order on the table. Maybe he hadn't seen anything suspicious in any of that or all of it combined. But I did. Why would anyone clean a handgun with a lighted cigarette in his hand or mouth? Cleaning fluid is flammable, for one thing. And you need clear eyes and both hands free throughout the process to do a proper job. It wasn't inconceivable that a distracted, obsessive man would make the mistake of lighting up; in fact, it could've been the cigarette that led to an accidental firing of the weapon—smoke getting in his eyes, hot ash dropping on his hand, that kind of thing. Still, it didn't feel right to me. None of it did. If he'd been sitting at or close to the table when the gun went off, the impact of the bullet would have kicked both him and the chair backward, toppled both to the floor. Chances were he'd have also whacked the table in reflex, sent some or all of the supplies toppling over and off. The fact that none of that had happened said to me he'd either been standing when the slug hit him, or he'd been perched on the edge of the bed—and it didn't make much sense that a man would stand up to clean a weapon, or sit to do the job five feet from where the supplies were . . .

The two women were watching me, Carmelita fidgeting and the older one in a kind of rigid, waiting-to-be-activated posture not unlike the vacuum cleaner. I smiled at them and said, "That's all, you can go back to work now," and plucked a pair of sawbucks out of my wallet and handed one to each woman. "*Mil gracias.*"

They looked at the money, at me, at each other. Their expressions were mirror images—an openmouthed mixture of incredulity and awe. An Anglo policeman who spoke Spanish, even if it was of the schoolbook variety, and handed out ten-dollar bills for no apparent reason? In their world, the not-so-brave new world of Los Estados Unidos, it was as much a miracle as any they were ever likely to encounter.

16

GEYSERVILLE. VILLAGE A DOZEN MILES or so north of Healdsburg, at the upper end of the Alexander Valley. Surrounded by wineries, vineyards, long stretches of flatland and low rounded hills. Tucked away in the hills were numerous mineral hot springs that gave the hamlet its name. Friend, fellow investigator, and licensed pilot Sharon McCone, who has flown over the area on her way to a Mendocino County retreat she shares with her significant other, once told me that from the air you can not only see and even smell steam rising from the underground springs, but also see a huge network of PG&E pipelines and energy-harnessing pumping stations. From ground level around Geyserville, though, your only view is of mostly pastoral countryside split by the concrete corridors of Highway 101.

The village is laid out along the east side of the freeway—a few dozen buildings, most flanking Geyserville Avenue and old enough to give the place a 1940s aspect that I found appealing. There were a couple of service stations, the one affiliated with the American Automobile Association, Kane's Towing and Service, on the south end. I'd found that out by calling Triple A from the car phone on my way up. The service truck and driver were out on a call when I rolled in at one-thirty; wouldn't be back until after two, the manager informed me. So I left the car there and walked back to the only restaurant, a well-regarded Italian place I'd eaten in a time or two, and killed forty minutes over a bowl of minestrone and some sourdough French bread. When I got back to the station, the tow truck was just pulling in.

The driver's name was Pete Flynn. Three or four years younger than me, with a substantial pot belly that made him seem bigger than he was and hair, eyebrows, and mustache all growing in wild tangles, like brush on a boulder. He was the garrulous type, always a fortunate draw when you're hunting information.

"Sure," he said, "I'm the guy took that call last week. Mule Deer Road, right?"

"Gail Kendall, two-fifteen Mule Deer Road." Tamara had gotten the address for me.

"Some name. The road, I mean. Ain't been a mule deer out that way in forty years. You another cop?" He grinned. " 'Scuse me, officer of the law."

"No. Private investigator."

"Yeah, huh? How come you're askin' same as the cops?"

"Insurance matter," I lied.

"Insurance," he said, as if it were a synonym for the next word out of his mouth. "Shit. One of 'em screwed my brother-in-law big time three years back. Fell off the roof of his house, up there puttin' new shingles on, busted both his legs and couldn't do nothing but sit around in a body cast for six months. Bastards wouldn't pay off. Said he was drunk. Hot day, man works through a six-pack or two, that ain't drunk. I ast you—you think that's drunk?"

"Depends on your brother-in-law's capacity for beer."

"Capacity? Put my money on Hank against all comers in a chuggin' contest. Buncha freakin' crooks, you ask me. Insurance companies."

"Some are worse than others," I said agreeably.

"But not yours, huh?"

"Mine, too. I work for more than one. Freelance."

"Then you ain't exactly one of 'em. Man's got to work, I don't hold that against nobody. What was it you wanted to ast me?"

"About the Kendall service call."

"What about it?"

"What time did she call in? Can you look up the exact time for me?"

"Don't have to look it up," Flynn said. "I remember on account of the sheriff's boys ast me when they come around. Eight-fifteen, ayem. On the nose."

Eight-fifteen. And Erskine had been shot at seven-forty. The timing, at least, didn't rule out Kendall as a suspect. I asked, "What time'd you get out to her house?"

"Musta been about eight-thirty. Left right away, takes maybe fifteen minutes to get to Mule Deer Road from here."

"And Gail Kendall was there waiting for you?"

"Sure. Out in the driveway, standin' next to her car. Ford Taurus. Piece of crap, the Ford Taurus. Buy American, I believe in that, I own a Chevvy myself, but a piece of crap is a piece of crap, no matter who makes it."

"The car had a dead battery, is that right?"

"Dead as hell. Couldn't raise a spark with the single cables. I hadda put the double jumpers on to get any juice."

Ridges appeared in the leathery skin of his forehead; he scratched his tangle of reddish hair with a dirty fingernail. "Funny thing, though."

"What is?"

"Bugger was old and corroded, older than the damn car, looked like. But she musta got a spark out of it in the garage before she called us."

"Why? Because the car was in the driveway?"

"Nah," Flynn said. "Engine and block was warm."

"As if the car'd been driven, you mean?"

"Yeah. Or set there idling for a while before the engine quit."

"And you say it was an old battery? Older than the car?"

"Looked that way to me. Could be the original conked out on her, too, and she had that one layin' around and stuffed it in there instead of buyin' a new one. Women and their cars. Jeez, you can't never tell what one of 'em will do to a set of wheels, even a piece of crap like the Ford Taurus. I remember one time—"

"Did you say anything to her about the battery? Mention the warm engine?"

"The battery—yeah. Told her she better get a new one or she'd be callin' us again because that old bugger wouldn't hold a charge. Only I didn't say bugger, not to her. Uh-uh."

"No?"

He winked. "Stone fox," he said. "Not that I cuss around any woman much, except my old lady, me bein' in the public service like I am, but around a stone fox I'm extra polite. That's just the way I am. I don't want the babes thinkin' I'm one of these crude guys don't give a Frenchman's fuck who they use shitty language to."

"You think Gail Kendall is a fox?"

"Sure. I got an eye for good-looking women. And them skinny types with the pouty lips put a charge in *my* battery, if you know what I mean."

I said, "Skinny?"

"Yeah, sure. Small, skinny, cute as a bug's ass."

"Pete, Gail Kendall is heavyset and thin-lipped."

"The hell she is. You musta never seen her, that's what you think."

"Or you saw somebody else," I said.

"Huh?"

"What color was her hair? What style?"

He shrugged. "Hey, man, hair's hair. I'm a leg and ass man myself. Hers looked pretty fine to me, what I could see under that heavy coat she was wearin'."

"Her hair, Pete. What color?"

"Couldn't tell you if I wanted to. She had this scarf tied around her head, covered up everything 'cept her face from the eyes down."

"How old was she?"

"Who knows from age? Old enough, that's for sure."

"Around forty?"

"Nah, not that old. Thirty, maybe. Yeah, around thirty."

"Wait here a second, okay? I'll be right back." I hustled over to my car. I'd put the photos of Janice Erskine in the glove compartment last week, after my first visit to Silver Creek Cellars, and they were still there. I brought the set back to Flynn. "Is this the woman you saw?"

He peered at one photo, then the other, turning each a little this way and that. Finally he said, "Could be."

"But you're not sure?"

"Could be. Got the same pouty lips. But this fox here, she's younger."

"Try to imagine her older by five years or so."

"I ain't got much imagination," Flynn said, but he tried. "Could be," he said.

"The woman on Mule Deer Road—how did she seem to you?"

"Huh?"

"Was she happy, nervous, upset—what?"

"I dunno, why?"

"It might be important, Pete. Think about it."

Thinking was a chore for him and it took him a while to get his memory cells in firing order. Then: "Kind of upset, I guess. Yeah. Wired, you know? She wouldn't hardly look at me, now I think about it."

"Kept her face averted? Turned away from you?"

"Yeah. I figured it was on account of I'm no Paul Newman. My face, some women like it and some don't, what the hell. Could be she was wired on account of the battery conkin' out and she's late for work. She said something about that when I got there, her bein' late for work."

"Did you tell any of this to the county cop you talked to? What the woman looked like, how she acted?"

"Nah, I don't think so."

"How about the old battery and the fact that the Ford's engine was warm when you got there?"

"Nah. They never ast me about none of that. You ast the right questions and they didn't."

That was it exactly. The key to finding out anything is whether or not you ask the right people the right questions.

I had no difficulty locating Mule Deer Road. It was off Lytton Springs Road southwest of Geyserville—a narrow country lane that wound back into the low hills and then began to climb. Near the top of a rise a driveway appeared, a narrow break in a stand of scrub oak; a mailbox on a post there bore the number 215 and the name "Kendall" in paste-on reflector orange.

The house and two outbuildings were partly visible as soon as you turned into the drive, spread along the flattened hilltop above. I drove up slowly, framing what I would say to Gail Kendall if I caught her home. It was probable that she'd be at the winery, but then, not everybody works a full eight hours on Friday. Safer for me if she was home, but I wouldn't be disappointed if she wasn't.

At the crest of the drive was a gravel parking area large enough to accommodate half a dozen vehicles. It was empty now and so was an extension of the drive that led to a detached garage separated from the house by a flower garden in full spring bloom. The house was smallish, of redwood and glass in no particular architectural style that I could identify. A raised redwood deck ran along the rear; from there you'd have an impressive view across the valley to the east, and of a miles-long stretch of the mountain range that extended north-south like the county's bony spine.

Nobody came out of the house when I parked or when I walked up onto a narrow front porch. And nobody responded to three long pushes on the doorbell. The screen door was unlatched, but a sturdy inner door was secure—almost a relief because I'd have been hard-pressed to resist the temptation of an unlocked door.

I stood listening to the wind mutter and bluster across the hilltop. It was strong up here, heavy with the scents of oak and sage, roses and climbing sweet pea and other blooms. Nice spot for a home, if you liked a certain isolation. I wondered if Gail Kendall had moved here from the Sonoma Valley to get away from people—a reaction to the hostage ordeal she'd gone through with her dead husband. Wondered, too, just how deeply the years and those final five hours with him had scarred her; if it had made her distrust men in general, and actively hate the abusers like Ira Erskine. If she was involved in Erskine's death, as I now believed, then the answer was yes. No sane and functional member of society conspires with a friend to commit murder, however powerful the motive, without some sort of intense personal impetus.

I went crunching across the gravel to the driveway extension. The garage was a short redwood-walled box, large enough for two cars to be squeezed in side by side, with a peaked sheet-metal roof that might have been added on as a rainy-season afterthought; the second outbuilding stood at the edge of the garden, a privy-size shed that no doubt held hoes and rakes and the like. The main garage door was locked and appeared to be electronically operated. I walked around to the near side, where a single door flanked by big, wheeled garbage containers was cut into the wall. That one was locked, too, but it wasn't much of a lock and the door was loose in the jamb. It wobbled and rattled when I tugged on the knob.

Here we go, I thought. And leaned my leg and hip tight against the lower half and did some strongarm lifting and yanking—what Kerry calls "animaling around"—and in less than thirty seconds, without my having to exert myself enough to break a sweat, the lock tore free of its plate and the door jerked open. There wasn't much damage: a little splintering of the wood around the plate, a bent edge, and some scrapes on the bolt. I ought to be able to relock it again when I was done inside. And the minor damage wouldn't be noticeable without a close examination.

Small surprise when I stepped into the inner gloom: a car was parked there. I found a light switch, and a bare overhead bulb chased away two-thirds of the shadows. White Ford Taurus—Gail Kendall's car. So where was she? Off with a friend, maybe. Or someone might have given her a ride to Silver Creek Cellars. In any event, for my purposes the presence of the car was an unexpected bonus.

I tried the driver's side door; it wasn't locked. I slid in and poked through the glove box without finding anything to hold my attention. A plastic trash bag hung from one of the radio knobs: used Kleenex, a candy wrapper, and a couple of styrofoam coffee containers. One of the tissues had a smear of bright-red lipstick—the shade Sondra Nelson had been wearing at Woolfox's ranch. I swept the floor mats in front and back, reaching under the seat as far as I could. Nothing.

Hood release, trunk release, and around back to check the trunk first. Nothing. I lifted the hood to have a look at the battery. Newish but not brand-new, the terminals free of acid-leak corrosion. It would be heavy to lift, but it was positioned where you could get at it easily enough; exchanging one battery for another would take less than five minutes, as long as you had a wrench handy and the rudimentary knowledge of how to hook up the cables. A woman could do it without much strain, even a small, slender woman like Sondra Nelson.

The old corroded battery Pete Flynn had recharged was still there in the garage, under a bench along the rear wall. I took a quick look, left it where it sat.

Finished. I stepped outside and futzed with the door until I was able to force the bolt back into the locking plate.

The house now? I wouldn't have minded a quick look around in there, but I was not going to break in to get it. Trespassing and animaling your way through a door into a garage were minor offenses; a house b&e was a major felony whether you took anything away with you or not. If Kendall happened to've left a window or the back door unlatched, maybe I'd chance it. Otherwise, no.

One other thing I could do here, even if it would make me feel like one of the government's dirty tricks boys. I lifted the lid on the nearest of the garbage containers, peered inside. Half full. I couldn't reach all the way down to the trash because the thing was a good five feet in height, so I tilted it carefully on its side and then got down on my knees and took off my jacket and rolled up my shirtsleeves and began sifting. Nasty job, and all it got me were stained fingers and an even lower opinion of myself. I almost didn't bother with the second container. Then I thought, what the hell, I'd gone this far, and opened that one and laid it down and went garbage-diving again.

Paydirt, partway through.

Perforated stub torn off a large postcard. I thought at first it was either part of a bill or some kind of computer-generated advertisement, but then I spotted the red lettering on the front: "Sonoma County, Office of the Jury Commissioner." Sondra Nelson's name was on it, too, along with a number—her assigned juror's number.

The stub went into my jacket pocket. And in my mind now was a developing idea of how they'd worked it. I needed a little more information to be sure the basic premise was possible; if it was, then I could go to Sheriff's Lieutenant Battle and lay it all out for him. He might not like the idea of my having conducted my own unsanctioned investigation, but he'd struck me as a dedicated cop without an ego problem, and that meant results were what counted with him.

Too late to get the information today? Probably, it being a Friday. If so, it could wait until Monday. Sondra Nelson and Gail Kendall weren't going anywhere.

I shoved the pile of smelly trash back inside and closed the container. I was about to wheel it back into its original position against the garage wall when I heard the sound rising above the cry of the wind. It froze me as soon as I recognized it.

A car was coming up the drive, whining in low gear.

17

I RAN THE GARBAGE CONTAINER OVER against the wall, twisted back to snatch up my jacket. There was just enough time for me to get it on before the car reached the top of the drive. Muddy brown Chrysler about ten years old, two people visible behind the windshield. When the driver saw me walking away from the garage he stood on the brakes hard enough for the front wheels to lock and the car to pull a quarter turn to the left before it stopped. I kept walking toward it, my hands in plain sight.

Five, six, seven seconds and then both doors flew open simultaneously. The driver was out first, moving fast—a burly guy in a corduroy jacket and Levi's. The passenger was Gail Kendall; she called out sharply, "Vic!" and swung around the open door, but the burly guy didn't slow or look back. His eyes were fixed on me and from the angry set of his mouth he already knew who I was.

I recognized him, too: the workman on the forklift I'd spoken to at the winery last Thursday. He plowed to a halt in front of me, blocking my way, and said heatedly, "What the hell're you doing here, man?"

I made the mistake of ignoring him, changing direction to bypass him on his left. He jumped over to block me again just as Kendall, running toward us, yelled his name a second time. I saw his arm swing up, but not in time to take evasive action; his fist smacked into my cheek, mashed my upper lip against my teeth. Pain erupted, my vision went cockeyed, and the next thing I knew I was down on my butt on the macadam with him standing over me, a kind of stolid elation on his face like a heavyweight who'd just fattened his ego on a tired old sparring partner.

Kendall loomed up at his side. "Vic, for God's sake, what's the matter with you? What did you hit him for?"

"He had it coming."

"What if he charges you with assault?"

"He's trespassing, ain't he?"

I was on one knee by this time. An incisor had sliced partway through the inside of my upper lip; I tasted blood, felt it trickling from a corner of my mouth. The punch had been solid enough but not square on or I'd have a worse cut and a couple of broken teeth. I shoved up onto my feet, spat out a gob of blood, smeared more of it off my mouth and over the back of one hand before I looked at Kendall and the burly guy again. He was still angry and she was halfway between anger and anxiety. Funny thing, but the knockdown hadn't built any rage in me. In a way, Vic was right: I'd had it coming.

"Okay," I said to him, "you win the round. But that's all it's going to be. One punch, one round."

"Yeah?"

"Yeah. You come at me again, I'll break something of yours."

"Tough talk for an old man."

"Come at me and we'll see how old I am."

Part of him wanted to push it; part of him didn't. The part with whatever sense he owned won out. He stood with his legs spread and his hands folding and unfolding at his sides, but he didn't do anything except glare at me. I let him maul me that way and turned my attention to Gail Kendall.

She said, "What're you doing on my property?"

"Looking for you."

"Why? What do you want this time?"

"Nothing much. A little talk."

"I don't have anything to say to you."

"Not to me, maybe."

". . . What does that mean?"

"Ira Erskine," I said.

Her anger was all but dead now, suffocating under the growing weight of anxiety. She wet her lips; her gaze wouldn't quite hold mine, as if she were afraid she might betray something through steady eye contact.

Vic said, still with heat, "He was in your garage, babe." The term of endearment stirred my memory and I heard him saying at the winery that he was Sondra Nelson's "best friend's main man." So Kendall wasn't a man-hater, just an abuse-hater.

"Is that right?" she said to me. "*Were* you in the garage?"

"No. Just looking around."

"For what?"

"Just looking around."

"Why don't we call the sheriff?" Vic said. "Trespassing's a crime, ain't it?"

"Why don't you shut up?" I said. "I'm talking to Ms. Kendall."

"Listen—"

"He's right, Vic. Be quiet." Then, to me, "I could do that. Call the county sheriff's office."

"Go ahead. Get Lieutenant Battle out here and the three of us will have a nice chat. About Erskine and the way he died."

"For God's sake," she said, almost plaintively, "why can't you just leave it alone? Leave Sandy alone. It was an accident—"

"Was it?"

"An *accident*. He was a miserable son-of-a-bitch, he hurt her badly and he would've killed her. He deserved what he got—"

"Like your husband nine years ago?"

Fresh anger darkened her eyes, bunched her face into a tight grimace. "You bastard," she said.

And all at once, looking at her, at Vic standing combatively at her side, I felt bad and sorry and sour about this whole business. It was as complicated, as hurtful to the survivors as Eberhardt's suicide was to its survivors, and here I was playing tough little mind games with a woman who'd suffered a kind of mental and physical anguish no man can fully understand. Never mind that she was almost certainly a co-conspirator in a premeditated homicide. She was also a victim, and who the hell was I to judge her anyway? Or Sondra Nelson or any other victim? I almost wished Vic would take another poke at me; if he did, I'd let him get away with that one, too. I was back to not liking myself again.

My mouth had started to hurt, the lip already to swell. I spat and wiped away more blood. "I'm sorry for that crack," I said to Kendall. "It was uncalled-for."

"You're still a dirty bastard," Vic said.

"Yeah. All right."

She said, "You think I had something to do with it, don't

you? Erskine's death. That's why you're sucking around."

I didn't say anything.

"You think what you want to about me, I don't care, but you leave Sandy alone. You hear me? You just let that poor woman try to pick up the pieces. She didn't have anything to do with him dying."

"Better leave Gail alone, too," Vic said, "or by Christ you and me'll tangle again."

Empty voices blowing in the wind. Silently I moved around past the two of them, walked slow along the drive and across to my car. There was a first-aid kit in the trunk, but I wouldn't treat my cut mouth here. Not here. I got in and started the engine and backed up and drove away without another glance at Gail Kendall and her boyfriend.

Sometimes you just can't look back.

Sometimes being right is a hell of a lot worse than being wrong.

I might've stopped at the Sonoma County courthouse on my way back through Santa Rosa, even though it was almost four o'clock, except that blood had dripped onto the front of my shirt and the sleeve of my jacket and by then my lip was swollen to double size. On the best of days my face has the appearance of a chunk of old limestone; in its present state it would frighten kids and old ladies, and make just about any county employee turn a deaf ear to the questions I needed answering.

Monday was soon enough. And the way I felt now, I was not even sure I wanted to come back then.

But I would. Like it or not.

The one thing I can never do, no matter what my personal feelings, is to turn my back on a problem before it's resolved one way or another.

* * *

I was sitting in my chair in Kerry's condo, cleaned up and more or less presentable, trying not to dribble beer onto Shameless who was curled up purring on my chest, when she arrived a little past seven. She said something flip about the prodigal returning, came over to give me a kiss. Bending, she spotted the fat lip, stared at it for a three-beat, and straightened again without touching me.

"Aren't you a little old to be getting into fights?" she said.

"Beginning to think I'm too old for a lot of things."

"Not one that comes to mind, thank God. What happened?"

"Nothing much. One-punch affair."

"It didn't have anything to do with Eberhardt, did it?"

"No. I was someplace I probably shouldn't've been and a guy didn't like it. Not his fault. He was defending his woman."

"From advances by you?"

"You know better than that."

"Uh-huh. Want to talk about it?"

"Yes, but not now. Not just yet."

"At your service, whenever. Does that lip need doctoring?"

"All taken care of. I could use another beer, though."

She went to the kitchen, came back with a can of Bud Light for me and a glass of white wine for herself. She kicked off her shoes, shed her suit jacket, and curled up on the couch. The cat eyed her, decided equal time was called for, made a happy burbling sound in his throat, jumped off my lap and bounded up onto hers.

She said, "I'm glad you're here. I missed you."

"You talking to me or Shameless?"

"You. He hasn't been absent for two-plus days."

"You ought to be happy I wasn't around. I haven't been fit company for anybody, including myself."

"Eberhardt," she said, and this time it wasn't a question.

"Yeah."

"And?"

I couldn't bring myself to talk about Eberhardt's shakedown of Danny Forbes, his corruption. Eventually I'd tell her, as I told her everything of any importance, but not just yet. I said, "I thought I had something with that ER doctor, Caslon, but it fizzled on me."

"Still no idea of what made him do it?"

"Faint glimmer, that's all."

"Maybe what you need is some time off," she said. "Eberhardt on top of what you went through in Creekside—circuit overload."

"Probably," I admitted. "Working too hard and not too well. I figured I'd try to drive Eberhardt out of my head by chasing another case, and all that got me was this fat lip and a dose of self-disgust. You want to hear me tell you again what a lousy profession I'm in?"

"No. How about this weekend?"

"How about what this weekend?"

"A short getaway, just the two of us. You don't have anything important on, do you?"

"Uh-uh. Free until Monday."

"Me, too. Sound good?"

"Very good. Where'll we go?"

"Up or down the coast. You choose."

"I'd rather you chose. Some romantic hideaway."

"Well . . . remember that little inn north of Gualala? Rocky headland, sea lions on the rocks, the beach with all the driftwood . . ."

"And the big fireplace in the room. I remember."

"I'll bet you do."

"That was some night, wasn't it?"

"Medicine for melancholy," she said. "Shall I call the inn, see if they have a room available for tomorrow?"

"If they do, try to get the same one as last time."

They did and she did. And I began to look forward to the trip. And to think that we really ought to do more of that kind of thing—not just overnight and two- or three-day getaways, but a week or ten days here, another week or ten days there. Actual vacations of the sort normal people take. We always had a good time, off somewhere alone together; and I was getting too old for the type of workaholic lifestyle I'd followed most of my life. Eberhardt's demise may have been self-generated, but a death from any cause is still a death. When people your own age, people you've known for decades, begin to die off it's time to step back a little, take a look at your own fragile existence. Time to start doing more to fill the years you have left than wallowing in pools of other people's misery. In the short and long runs both, that was the most effective of all the medicines for melancholy.

18

BEFORE WE LEFT IN THE MORNING I called the office and accessed the answering machine, just in case any urgent messages had come in Friday afternoon. Tamara works part-time some Fridays, depending on her school schedule; she hadn't been in yesterday at all. I was aware of a certain irony as I made the call, after last night's avowal to back off on work, spend more time smelling the roses. But you can't hurl yourself into a lifestyle change all at once— at least I couldn't. Do it gradually, wean myself away from the work-as-number-one-motivator mindset, and I'd be much more likely to stick to my resolve. Besides, there was still the Erskine business to be dealt with. And Eberhardt, like a small tumor that somehow had to be cut out before any real healing could begin.

There were two messages on the machine, both from the same party: Sondra Nelson. One late yesterday afternoon, one at nine this morning. Both said essentially the same thing. Please call her as soon as possible, it was important she talk to me; she would be at the winery all day today, in the afternoon tomorrow, all day again on Monday. She sounded controlled, businesslike, but there was an undercurrent in both messages that I took to be fear. Source: Gail Kendall. They'd had a conference, decided it was Nelson who stood the best chance of finding out how much I knew and of trying to sway or dissuade me. She wanted me to contact her at Silver Creek so her fiancé wouldn't be involved, which fit with my suppositions. Erskine's murder was a two-person job, and James Woolfox wasn't one of the two.

I rang up the winery, and she came on the line in a hurry. "Yes, hello," she said. "Thank you for getting back to me so promptly."

"What can I do for you, Ms. Nelson?"

"Well, I wonder—Could you hold a moment?" She went away for about fifteen seconds. Closing an office door or switching phones for privacy, I thought. "I'm back," her voice said in my ear. "I wonder if we could talk in person, privately? Either up here or in the city, if you prefer."

Uh-huh, I thought. Did I owe Sondra Nelson the courtesy of another meeting? Yes. I felt sorry for her and Gail Kendall, in spite of or maybe because of what they'd felt compelled to do, and there was no denying that I was partly responsible for putting her in a position where she had had to make that kind of choice. But the meeting would not go as she and Kendall hoped it would. If there was any swaying done, I'd be the one to do it.

I said, "I think that can be arranged. When did you have in mind?"

"As soon as possible. Today?"

"Can't be done. I'm about to leave for the weekend. I won't be available until Monday."

Longish pause. "Monday morning?"

"Afternoon would be better. I have some business in the morning."

"All right. Where shall we meet?"

"The winery. Or anywhere in Sonoma County. I'll be in Santa Rosa, if you want to come there."

"Oh? Are you . . . you wouldn't be seeing Lieutenant Battle, would you?"

"Not before you and I talk."

Another pause. "Would you mind coming here? Santa Rosa . . . well, there're just too many people."

"I don't mind. Say one o'clock?"

"Yes." The throat-clearing sound again. "There'll be people here, too," she said. "At the winery proper. But there's another place on the property, the ruins of an old stone farmhouse. Would it be all right if I met you there?"

Dangerous games, Ms. Nelson? But I doubted it. She wouldn't play them on Woolfox's land, where he might be hurt by the backlash, and she couldn't be sure I hadn't already confided in Battle. Besides, I didn't see her as the sort who would always resort to violence when threatened. She was a victim, not an aggressor.

"How do I get to the farmhouse?"

She told me. It was only three-quarters of a mile from Silver Creek Cellars and I would have to go through the winery grounds to get there.

"If I'm held up in Santa Rosa for any reason," I said, "I'll call and let you know."

She said, "Thank you" before she broke the connection, but not in response to what I'd said. As if I'd given her something—a slender thread of hope, maybe.

Had I given her a thread of hope? I hadn't meant to. Whatever she had to say, it wouldn't make any difference in what I did. Murder was murder; motives and extenuating circumstances and emotional pleas didn't matter. Neither did pity nor compassion. If she was guilty, and I was sure she was, it was my duty to see that she was held accountable. Convince her to turn herself in, if I could; and if I couldn't, turn her and Gail Kendall in myself.

The drive up Highway 1, the stay at the little bluffside inn near Elk in Mendocino County, was a definite tonic. We walked on the beach, watched the sea lions playing among the offshore rocks, ate too much, built a pine-log blaze in a fireplace so large a hermit could have called it home, drank two bottles of an Alexander Valley cabernet not made by Silver Creek Cellars ("luscious fruit flavor, elegant balance, strong finish"), and got tight enough to engage in some moderately outrageous lovemaking on the carpet in front of the fire—outrageous, that is, for a none-too-svelte sixtyish Italian guy and a younger and considerably more mature stone fox. On Sunday we drove up the coast toward Little River, stopped in at Sharon McCone's retreat, Touchstone, to see if she and Hy Ripinsky were in residence—they weren't—and then headed back through the Anderson Valley, where we stopped at a couple of wineries to taste their reds and whites. Getting into it, by God. Before long we'd be subscribing to the *Wine Spectator*, using phrases like "delightful nose" and "resonant on the palate" with a straight face, and talking about establishing our own cellar.

Nice two days. Very.

I didn't think once about the Erskine case. Even Eberhardt's ghost pretty much left me alone.

First stop Monday morning: the office, to check the mail and finish up preliminary work on the insurance fraud case. Tamara came in all chipper and glowing again—another hot weekend with her symphonic hardman. I let her tell me a little about it, but when she started on the ins and outs—literally—of Mr. Mighty's canine testicular implant, I performed a successful verbal neutering operation on her. She wanted to know how I'd got the still-noticeable fat lip; I gave her a brief and ambiguous explanation, because I wasn't ready or willing to share the details on the Erskine homicide, and then changed the subject to the Mendocino trip. She allowed as how the weekend had been just what I needed, since I no longer looked like something Mr. Mighty might try to bury. And so it went. Typical sedate and respectful employer-employee conversation, as must surely go on in business offices throughout the city on any given Monday morning.

I was out of there by ten, and once again on the hunt for a parking place within reasonable proximity of the Sonoma County courthouse at eleven-fifteen. The one I found this time required a walk of no more than a third of a mile. It was warm in Santa Rosa today, a balmy spring day for one of the few instances this spring, and I enjoyed the walk. I even managed to hoof it up to the second floor of the courthouse without aggravating my sore back—a lingering reminder that men my age ought to be more careful when indulging in a Saturday-night bacchanal.

The woman in the jury commissioner's office was cooperative enough, though she would only answer nonspecific questions about the county's jury selection procedures; information on individual jurors was not to be given out. No problem there. The answers I did get were sufficient to bolster my suspicions. I would've liked to talk to the judge and members of the seated jury on the gang-rape trial Sondra Nelson had been called for; that might have produced some hard evidence in the form of a witness with a sharp memory.

But the trial had ended Friday morning, I was told, and the presiding judge was not in chambers today. Just as well. That sort of evidence-gathering was better handled by Lieutenant Battle and the county prosecutor's office.

The good feeling left over from the weekend was mostly gone by the time I got back to the car. I felt only marginally better, in fact, than I had on Friday afternoon. When you're carrying a couple of loads like Eberhardt's suicide and Ira Erskine's murder, two-day getaways are in a class with the generally accepted falsehood about Chinese food: the appeasing effects just don't last very long.

I consoled myself with the thought that in a few hours I would be free of the Erskine mess. One down, one to go.

19

THERE WERE HALF A DOZEN CARS parked at Silver Creek Cellars this afternoon, a knot of visitors in front of the tasting room entrance, even a young couple having a fair-weather picnic at a bench under one of the old live oaks. I envied them. The weekend in Mendocino seemed long past now, a memory that was already starting to blur at the edges.

Uphill beyond the warehouse was the vineyard road Sondra Nelson had told me to take; I drove that way, leaving the good and easy life behind. The road was in decent repair, hardpan overlain with gravel, but it ran an irregular route over and around rises and down through little swales and I couldn't make much time. The rows of grapevines were tall, their leaves a chlorophyll green color that had a fresh-scrubbed shine in the sunlight. I passed a trio of laborers working among the rows; they stopped to watch curiously as I clattered by. At three-tenths of a mile by the odometer, the road hooked right and blended into another, slightly wider one that climbed into low hills. Old farm road, this one. The shallow, brush-banked creek that paralleled it on the south was probably the same one that ran behind the winery buildings.

The road took me up a moderately steep hillside, at the top of which the vast acreage of vineyards ended, and then dropped me down into a shallow bowllike valley. The three or four acres of flatland looked as though they had once been cultivated—hay, alfalfa, maybe hops—but that had been many years ago; now they were coated in grass and weeds and an encroaching section of wild mustard. Ahead, as I descended, I could see an old wooden bridge spanning the creek, and close beyond that, along the bank and partially screened by willows and aspens, the remains of the farm buildings.

I turned onto the bridge, thumped over its warped boards. The farmhouse was a tumbledown stone shell so overgrown with grass, bushes, wild berry vines, and climbing primroses that it seemed to be sinking inexorably into the earth. To one side, at the rear, was a huge jumble of weathered boards and one leaning wall, all that remained of a barn. A dark blue Lexus was drawn up between the house and the former barn, in what had once been a garden of some sort. I couldn't see the front half of it from my angle of approach, but Sondra Nelson was probably waiting inside. The only outward sign of life on the property were a couple of birds having a mating argument on what was left of the house's roof.

I pulled up just across the bridge. And the first thing I noticed then was the line of the creek coming out of the trees to the west, the willows and aspens stark against the sky. It was this scene that had been the inspiration and model for Sondra Nelson's Silver Creek Cellars label.

The view held my attention for a bit. When I turned my

head again I had company: Sondra Nelson was coming my way from the Lexus, and she wasn't alone. She'd brought Gail Kendall along for backup.

It didn't have to mean anything one way or another, but when you're meeting somebody in an out-of-the-way place like this and the prearrangements turn out to be altered, it makes you wary. A touch paranoid, too. I leaned over and flipped the spring catch that holds the .38 Colt Bodyguard I keep under the dash; slipped the weapon from its hooks and slid it inside my belt on the right side, under my jacket where it wouldn't show. Better to give in to a little paranoia than to get caught unprotected.

The birds were still making a racket as I exited the car, lunging and screeching at each other in a flurry of wings. Rough sex in the animal kingdom. Nelson and Kendall slowed as I moved toward them, so that when the three of us met it was in front of the broken and half-hidden farmhouse porch. Nelson wore a lined windbreaker over an ankle-length skirt, the jacket zipped to the throat and her hands in the pockets and her shoulders hunched as if she were cold. Kendall was in Levi's and a plaid Pendleton. Tension was like an adhesive in both their faces, binding them into unnaturally stiff expressions. Anger burned in the older pair of eyes; the younger pair was bleak, caught halfway between resignation and desperation.

I said to Sondra Nelson, "I thought this was supposed to be a two-person meeting."

"Coming along was my idea," Kendall said. "I didn't want Sandy seeing you alone."

"Afraid she'd say something she shouldn't?"

"No."

"United front?"

"That's right. How much do you want?"

". . . What?"

"You heard me. How much to quit investigating us, leave us alone once and for all?"

"Are you trying to buy me off?"

"Oh for God's sake," she said, "why else would you be doing this? Let's just get it out into the open."

"I'm not the one who asked for this meeting—"

"You would have sooner or later. How much?"

"I'm not for sale, Ms. Kendall."

"Everybody's for sale at the right price."

"Not everybody." My name isn't Eberhardt, I thought. You can't buy my soul for five hundred pieces of silver and two bottles of Jack Daniel's. "I never had any intention of blackmailing either of you."

Nelson said plaintively, "Then why are you persecuting us?"

"Persecuting, Ms. Nelson?"

"Investigating on your own when the county sheriff . . . They're satisfied, why aren't you?"

"Don't be so sure Lieutenant Battle is satisfied."

"He hasn't bothered us again," Kendall said. "But you . . . is it because you worked for Erskine?"

"No."

"Don't tell me you sympathized with him. You think he had a right to come after Sandy, tear her life apart?"

"No. Nobody has that right."

"Then why? What do you expect to get out of it?"

"How about a little justice?" I said.

"Justice! For a piece of shit like Ira Erskine?"

"He was a human being, no matter how miserable an excuse for one. And he was murdered in cold blood."

"You don't know that."

"Don't I?"

"You don't *know* anything."

Sondra Nelson said, "If we could only make you understand—"

"Understand what?"

"What a monster he was. How frightened I was."

"You ran away from him once, changed your name, started over. You could've done it again."

"No. No, I couldn't."

"Of course she couldn't," Kendall said. "The man she loves, everything she ever wanted is right here in this valley. How long do you think a person can go on living in terror of her life?"

"You lived that way for a lot of years, didn't you?"

Her gaze raked my face. "I was a fool," she said. "Sandy and I were both fools. The only way to deal with vermin—"

"—is to exterminate them."

"Well? You said it, I didn't."

"I said it, but the two of you did it. Whose idea, Ms. Kendall? Yours?"

"You don't know a damn thing," she said, but this time as if she were trying to convince herself.

"I know the two of you conspired to kill Ira Erskine. And I know how you did it—the double switch, the whole plan."

Nelson moaned, "Oh, God . . ."

"Hush, Sandy, it's all right. He can't prove whatever he thinks he knows." The hot eyes scorched me again. "There's no proof we did anything, either of us."

"But there is," I said. "Enough to have both of you charged with at least second-degree homicide."

"You're so fucking smart. Go ahead, then, tell us. How'd we do it? What's your proof?"

Laying it out in detail was about the only chance I had of convincing them to turn themselves in. I still felt sorry for both of them, despite Kendall's combative attitude; and whether or not they believed it, I hated this as much as they did and I was suffering right along with them.

"All right," I said. "Last Sunday in the Napa Valley—that's when you planned it, the two of you alone somewhere. The problem was to get rid of Erskine quickly and in a way that left you both in the clear. Solution: a double switch to create two solid alibis. On Monday morning you traded cars and places. You drove down to Santa Rosa to take Ms. Nelson's place on jury duty, she went to Healdsburg to shoot her ex-husband and then back to Geyserville to pretend to be you stranded at home."

If I needed any further confirmation that I was right, Sondra Nelson's anguished face gave it to me. But Kendall said scornfully, "That's ridiculous. How could I possibly take Sandy's place on jury duty?"

"Easily enough in Sonoma County. When you're selected here you receive a computer-generated postcard that you take with you on the day you're to serve. The card comes in two parts, perforated, both of which have your name and juror's number on it. You tear off one part and put it in a box when you arrive, then go into the jury room and wait for your number to be called. Meanwhile, a clerk in the commissioner's office checks the stubs against a master list to make sure the summoned person is present. That's all—nobody checks individual ID at any time. No reason to; it's almost unheard of for one person to take on someone else's jury duty."

"Sandy was called for a rape trial that morning. She was almost seated—"

"Her *number* was called. Everything is done by juror number—pool selection for a particular trial, individual selection for the jury. The judge or lawyers ask the called juror's name and some general personal history, but you could answer those questions as easily as she could. And it wasn't hard to talk yourself out of being seated. Plenty of ways to do that—claimed you were a rape victim yourself, or had a family member who was raped, or simply said you had a strong antirape bias and couldn't be impartial. Once a juror is excused, that's pretty much it unless the trial docket is heavy and the general jury pool thin for one reason or another, and those weren't the cases on Monday. Out of the courtroom, out of the courthouse, and home free.

"And while you were handling things in Santa Rosa, Ms. Nelson drove your car to the Pinecrest Motel, talked her way into Erskine's room, used her wiles to—"

Nelson: "No!"

"—to throw him off guard, got her hands on his gun, and shot him. She couldn't go back out through the door because the shot had brought witnesses, so she wriggled out through the bathroom window, slipped around front to where your car was parked, and drove away. Somewhere between Healdsburg and Geyserville she stopped to call Triple A, using your name and card number and a public phone so the call couldn't be traced. Straight to your house then, where she pulled another switch—the old corroded battery from the garage into the Ford in place of the good one. When the serviceman showed up and put in a charge in the old battery, she signed off as Gail Kendall and reswitched the batteries once he was gone. And then waited for you to return from Santa Rosa to reclaim her car."

Neither woman spoke when I finished. The silence had a heavy, swollen quality; even the mating birds were still. Sondra Nelson was so pale I could see the fine tracery of veins in her cheeks; the bright-red lipstick she wore made her mouth look bloody. The older woman hated me with an unblinking intensity, as if by sheer force of will she might manage to make me keel over dead at their feet.

She ended the silence by saying, "You're so goddamn smug, aren't you?" in a choked voice.

"Smug, Ms. Kendall?"

"Smug and self-righteous. Sees all, knows all. Well, you're not half as smart as you think you are."

"Experienced and methodical, not smart. You're mistaken if you think I'm enjoying this."

"But that hasn't stopped you, has it?"

"From doing my job? No."

"Ruining people's lives. That's some job."

"I didn't conspire to kill Ira Erskine. The two of you did that."

"You can't prove it."

"You keep saying that. But I don't have to prove it. That's up to Lieutenant Battle and the county prosecutor. And I wasn't bluffing about there being enough evidence to have you both indicted."

"*What* evidence?"

"The Triple-A driver can identify which of you was at your house that morning. And I found the other portion of the jury summons, the one you kept, buried in your garbage. There're other things, too. And more to be found with a little digging."

"You haven't talked to Battle yet. Why not?"

"It'll go easier on you if you confess. That's why I agreed to come here—to give Ms. Nelson, and you, a chance to go to him first."

"And if we don't?"

"You know the answer to that."

"Doesn't it matter to you *why*? Any of the reasons why? Don't you have any compassion?"

"More than you might think."

"But not enough. Even though you're right about only part of it. The rest . . . you couldn't be more wrong."

"What part am I wrong about?"

"Tell him, Sandy. Tell him what really happened in that motel room."

Sondra Nelson jerked a little, as if she'd been touched with a live, low-voltage wire. She said, "No, I can't go through all that again. What's the use? It won't matter to him, he doesn't care . . ."

"Tell him anyway. I want to see his face."

There was another period of silence, more charged than before. A breeze had kicked up and was rustling the trees, bringing the smell of green things growing and the vagrant scent of apple blossoms even though no apple trees were visible in the vicinity.

"Suppose . . ." Nelson began, and stopped and cleared her throat, passed a hand over her eyes to clear them, too. "Suppose we did plan to kill Ira, just as you said. Planning something like that and actually going through with it . . . they're not the same. Even if you know it's the only way to save your life, he's still someone you once loved, had a child with. It's not easy . . . it's not . . . you can't . . ."

She was trembling by then. Her eyes, round and moist, were like those of a spotlighted deer.

"Suppose I did go to his motel to . . . end the fear. With my own gun, one I've had for years for protection, in my purse. And suppose I took it out once I was in the room and pointed it at him, and he stood there looking at me in that arrogant way of his and saying, 'You can't do it, Janice, you can't shoot me.' And he was right, I couldn't . . . I tried, I wanted to, but I . . ." Pause, her throat working, her face paper-white except for red splotches spreading slowly, like patches of spilled blood, across her cheekbones. "And suppose he took my gun away from me, pulled it out of my hand and put it back in my purse and then he . . . suppose he . . . stepped up close, smiling the whole time, and hit me hit me hit me and threw me down on the bed and hit me and took my clothes off, not tore them off, *took* them off, oh he was very tender then, as if it was our wedding night, and tender when he raped me, all the while whispering how much he loved me and exactly how he would kill me if I didn't go back to Santa Fe with him . . ."

Ragged breath, and then the rest of it in the past tense, without qualifiers, her eyes squeezed shut and her voice congealed: "Afterward he went into the bathroom and I crawled off the bed and managed to put on my clothes, and his gun was lying there on the table, and I picked it up, and he came out of the bathroom wearing his robe and smiled at me as if nothing terrible had happened, as if it was perfectly normal, and said 'I love you, Janice,' just like that, and went over and picked up his cigarettes from the nightstand and lighted one, and I walked around in front of him and I . . . he looked at me and saw the gun and he said, 'Oh Christ, Janice, not this again' and I . . . the gun . . . his head just seemed to . . . I couldn't look at him lying on the floor, all the blood . . . outside there were voices and somebody pounding on the door . . . I couldn't think, I ran into the bathroom . . ."

She sagged a little as the last of it dribbled out. Gail Kendall caught her arm, held her with a kind of fierce protectiveness.

Dry-mouthed, I asked, "If you were so distraught, why

did you close the window after you were out? Make sure the catch was fastened?"

"I don't know, I don't remember anything about that. I was in the bathroom and then I was outside and then I was in Gail's car driving away. It's all . . . fragmented. Unreal, as if it were happening to somebody else."

I had nothing to say to that.

Kendall said, "You don't believe her, do you?"

"Why should I? The story's convincing, she's convincing, but so was Erskine the day he poured out his lies to me. I swallowed that sob story, but I'm not swallowing any more without corroboration."

"Corroboration," Sondra Nelson said in a dull voice. "All right, if that's what you want."

She pushed away from the older woman, unzippered her windbreaker. And then in a series of swift movements she opened her skirt and let it fall, caught the waistband of a pair of white briefs and yanked them partway down, and with her other hand lifted the blouse to her breasts—exposing the entire middle of her body.

Healing scrapes and welts, bruises still purple-black and piss-yellow at the edges. From sternum to crotch, a madman's abstract design hammered out on human flesh.

"Well?" Kendall said savagely. "*Now* do you believe her?"

I'd seen and heard enough, too much. All of a sudden there were too many conflicting emotions swirling around inside me. I turned away from the two of them. Walked toward my car, not fast and not slow. I could feel the .38 inside my belt, the barrel digging into my hipbone, the grip tight against the pad of fat above. It felt like a dirty hand—Ira Erskine's hand.

Hard steps behind me, hurrying to catch up. Hard fingers

gripping my arm to halt me before I reached the car. Gail Kendall in my face again. "Are you going to see Battle now?"

". . . No. Not now."

"But eventually. You'll still turn us in."

"I don't know."

"We'd never be convicted, you know we wouldn't. No jury would ever convict two battered women in a case like this. I don't care about myself, but Sandy . . . you'd be putting her through more hell for nothing. *Nothing!*"

I shook my head. It had a loose feel on the stem of my neck.

"Hasn't she suffered enough? You heard her, she's sick about what he made her do. She'll never get over it. Isn't that punishment enough?"

"She killed a man," I said, only this time it sounded hollow—a meaningless phrase in a legal brief, words blowing in the wind.

"Not a man," Kendall said, "a rabid dog like the one I lived with for ten years. She killed a rabid dog to save her life, the same as the county SWAT team killed one to save mine."

"You'll hear from me. I won't do anything without letting one of you know first." I started moving again.

"When?" she said behind me. "*When?*"

I had no answer for her; I had no answer for myself. All I could do at this point, all I did, was to get into the car and drive the hell away from there.

20

"I THOUGHT I HAD IT ALL FIGURED when I went out there," I said to Kerry. "Cut-and-dried, and no matter what Sondra Nelson said it wouldn't make any difference. But when I heard and saw what he'd done to her, those bruises . . . it did something to me. Now it doesn't seem half as simple as it did before."

"He must've been a monster. Erskine."

"Yeah. But I already knew that . . . Oh, hell, I don't know. I just feel bad for both of them. Smug and self-righteous, Kendall called me, and she was right. I paid lip service to having compassion, but I didn't take enough of it out there with me."

"Are you saying you're sorry you found out the truth?"

"Christ, no. I'd feel twice as bad if I'd heard it later, after I dumped my version on Battle."

The water in the tub was cooling; I turned the hot water tap on full blast again. Steam rose in thick floating layers that gave Kerry, seated on the clothes hamper across the bathroom, an ethereal quality, as if I were talking to an ectoplasmic representation rather than a real person.

She said, "You are going to tell him, aren't you?"

"I don't know yet. I still haven't made up my mind."

"You will," she said.

"Will I? What makes you so sure?"

"Because you know they won't confess of their own volition and Battle probably won't find out without your help. There's nobody else to see that justice is done."

"Honorable, dutiful, Mr. Do-the-Right-Thing."

"That's you. You couldn't let two people get away with murder."

"I'm not so sure about that."

"Compromise your principles, jeopardize your career, for a pair of strangers—?"

"A pair of badly used human beings." My principles aren't exactly what they used to be, either, I thought, but I kept that to myself. "Kerry, what would you have done in Sondra Nelson's place?"

"Come on, that's not a relevant question."

"It's relevant to me. Suppose that screwball ex of yours was stalking you—"

"Ray? He may be crazy, but he was never abusive."

"All right, but suppose he was and he'd been stalking you ever since you left him. And he found you and threatened your life in front of witnesses and you knew he meant it. Would you throw away the new life you'd built, a man you loved and who loved you, and start running and living in fear again? Or would you take desperate action?"

"I can't answer that," Kerry said. "No woman can, really, unless she's living in such a situation."

"Right. Exactly. You get pushed to the limits and then

you find out. So it *is* possible you'd've done just what Sondra Nelson did. You don't rule it out."

"I doubt I could kill anyone."

"Not even if you were beaten and raped? Not even to save your own life?"

"In self-defense, yes. I came close to doing just that not so long ago, don't forget."

"I'll never forget that night in Cazadero."

"Premeditated murder, though . . . no, I couldn't plan and carry out a cold-blooded act like that. Not many people could."

"Neither could Nelson. That's central in her case. She didn't shoot him until he beat and raped and threatened her again. And when he did those things, he made it self-defense."

"You're splitting hairs," Kerry said. "She went to the motel with the intention of killing him. She admitted that she tried to do it when she got there."

"But she didn't. Besides, does self-defense always have to be spontaneous to qualify? Always, in every case?"

"Maybe not. But taking a human life is still wrong."

"So Nelson and Kendall should be punished."

"Yes."

"Because the law says so."

"Well?"

"Even if they could be convicted," I said, "and Kendall was right that it isn't likely, what purpose would be served? Who'd benefit from them going to prison, two essentially law-abiding women who're no longer a threat to any individual or to society at large?"

"How can you be sure they're no longer a threat? What if somebody else harasses one or both of them? If they got away with murder once, they might be inclined to try it again."

"I don't think so. Erskine was the psychopath, not Nelson or Kendall."

"You could be wrong."

"I could be, sure. No absolutes."

"Except for our laws—they're the closest to absolutes we have. If there wasn't punishment for people who break them, what good would they be? You might as well have anarchy."

"No argument there. But what's more important, punishment or justice? The two aren't always synonymous. The law isn't always inviolable, no matter what the legal profession would have us believe, and justice isn't always best served by legal interpretation."

"Now you're rationalizing."

"Maybe."

"Or worse, thinking of playing God."

"Babe," I said, "judges and lawyers and juries play God every day. Strangers who know little and care less about the individuals they sit in judgment of. You think they always play strictly by the rules? That they don't manipulate and maneuver and rationalize and exercise personal prejudice and deliberately misinterpret facts simply because they're empowered by the legal system? That's another illusion we keep fooling ourselves with. We *all* play God sometimes. And sometimes the God we play is more just than the God the lawmakers play."

She sat quiet. The steam had dissipated again and I could see her face clearly. The frown she wore said she was doing a little God-playing herself at the moment, sitting in judgment of me and my heretical argument.

"Besides," I said, "I'm the one who put Erskine in a position to harm his ex-wife, and her in the position of having to defend herself against him. So if I do decide to keep what I know to myself, all I'd be doing is reversing myself on the judgment seat. Trying to be a better God-player than I was before."

"You really believe that? Everything you've been saying?"

"Fundamentally. And if you're going to say that I'd be putting myself above the law, that's not true. I'm bound by it and a slave to it just like everybody else, and you know I wouldn't have it any other way. What we're talking about here is interpretation by one man in one specific case. My interpretation of justice here doesn't necessarily coincide with the the laws of California. That's the bottom line."

"So you're going to do it. Let those women get away with murder."

"I didn't say that. I told you, I still haven't made up my mind. All I know right now is, I can't stop thinking about Sondra Nelson and what that son-of-a-bitch did to her. I can't get the image of all those bruises out of my mind . . ."

I went to bed early, dropped off right away—more a passing out than a falling asleep, as tired as I was—and immediately dreamed the Eberhardt dream. *Join me for a midnight snack?* And then dreamed it again. *Let's eat.* And kept on dreaming it, as if it were a phantasmic snake rolling on and on while it tried to gobble its own tail.

Join me for a midnight snack?

Corner ahead, just come around the corner . . .

I was sitting up in bed. Wide awake, with no sense of transition between unconscious and conscious.

Beside me, Kerry stirred and made a disturbed sound, but she didn't wake up. The bedside clock read 3:11.

My mind was fuzzy at the edges but clear and sharp in the

center, as though I were looking at something far away through a telescopic lens and the magnification brought it up close in all its detail. There was sweat on my neck and throat as I examined it. The palms of my hands felt moist.

I sat there.

Ask the right questions, you get the right answers. Look at something long enough and in the right way, dreams included, and all the distortions and blockages disappear and you see it for what it really is. Open up your mind and the light, too damn much light, shines in.

I sat a while longer, then got up and used the bathroom. Came back and lay down beside Kerry and listened to the gentle rhythm of her breathing.

Jesus, I thought, please let me be wrong about *all* of it this time.

But I knew I wasn't.

I stayed in bed later than usual for a weekday morning, letting Kerry get up first. She brought me coffee, tried to make conversation and gave it up when she saw that my mind was elsewhere. A kiss, a lingering whiff of the spicy perfume she favored, and she was gone. I hauled myself out of the warm nest and showered and drank more coffee, killing time until the kitchen clock showed that it was past nine. Then I was out of the condo to start my day.

Another bad one. Even worse than yesterday.

At San Francisco General I avoided the ER and went up to the administration wing instead. This was Tuesday and Dr. Caslon was off on Tuesdays, but I no longer needed him to answer questions for me. A Chinese woman in the billing department took care of that chore. All it required were a couple of glib lies and the dropping of a name that wasn't my own.

Right questions, right answers.

Running on the right track at last—and wishing I could get off before the finish line.

My flat.

The scattered piles of Eberhardt's office records, a quick hunt through them for his final Cellular One bill. And there it was, the last charge, the last call—the last piece of proof.

So that part of it was clear and irrefutable. I could still be off the beam on the other part, the way I'd been off on what had happened in the Pinecrest Motel room a week ago yesterday—not much but enough to make the truth a little less repellent, a little more tolerable.

Slowly I got up from the desk and slowly I went into the bedroom to the phone.

In the car again, driving.

Too-familiar route the past few days, and wouldn't you know that traffic would be light. It never seemed to be that way when you were in a hurry.

Thirty-eight-minute trip. I marked the passage of each on the dashboard clock, hating every one.

21

SHE WAS WAITING FOR ME ON THE porch, in the shade of the big magnolia tree. Wearing a lightweight, butterscotch-colored suit and a peach-hued blouse, all of which seemed to hang shapelessly on her thin body the way clothing hangs on a scarecrow. When I'd talked to her at the San Rafael real estate brokerage company—she'd gone back to work last week—she had thought at first that I was after her again about the uncashed five-hundred-dollar check. No, I said, I needed to talk to her right away on another matter, and not at her office or any other public place. And she'd said, "Home, then," in a voice gone as dull and lifeless as it had been during that painful Sunday visit nine days ago. Meaning her temporary home, the only one she had now—the Hoyt house in Ross.

When I came up onto the porch she was on her feet and smiling, but there was no warmth or light in the smile. It was nothing more than a narrow stretching and upturning, like the stitched grin on the face of a rag doll. A pale-skinned rag doll with hollow cheeks and spectral eyes.

"You made good time," she said with false cheerfulness. "I've only been here two or three minutes."

"Not much traffic."

"We can talk inside or out here . . ."

"Doesn't matter."

"Out here, then. The weather's been so nice the past couple of days." She sat down again in a padded redwood armchair. I leaned a hip against the porch railing; I didn't feel like sitting. "Spring has always been my favorite time of year."

I had no comment on that.

"I hope this won't take long, I can't take more than an hour for lunch and it's twelve-thirty already—" She broke off abruptly, and the stitched grin vanished and the shape of her expression changed, darkened. "Oh God," she said, "I knew when you started asking all those questions it would come to this. The five hundred dollars, the psychologist, the emergency room doctor . . ."

"He was abusing you, wasn't he, Bobbie Jean?"

The question seemed to hang in the air between us. She sat still so long it was as if the essence of her had gone away, leaving nothing but the shell of her body. Then, not quite looking at me, "How did you know?"

The way you moved at the funeral, stiff and slow—the same way Sondra Nelson moved that day at Woolfox's ranch. The labored breathing, the winces—as if there might be bruises under your clothing, too. But all I said was, "How long?"

"Physically? Not long."

"Weeks, months?"

"A few weeks. Before that, it was all words, looks, gestures . . . you know."

"Yeah, I know."

"It wasn't much at first. A shove, a slap, a poke in the arm. But then it was happening every time he drank too much, every time we had a cross word about alcohol or money or any of the other things we fought over. He grew angrier, and the slaps and pokes harder and harder. I could see he was losing control. Of his work, his life, everything."

"What did you do about it?"

"Tried to convince him to stop drinking, join AA, see a doctor. I threatened to leave him. Once I even threatened him with legal action. None of it did any good. It only made matters worse."

"You could have left him."

"I tried that, too. More than once I had my mind made up and my bags packed. The only time I actually put them in the car, he came after me and begged me to stay. Down on his knees, crying like a little boy, telling me how much he needed me. I couldn't turn my back on him. I should have, I know that, but I couldn't."

Foul taste in my mouth again; I worked saliva through it before I asked, "What happened that last Sunday night, two weeks ago? The night you ended up in the hospital?"

"Another argument, a whole flock of vicious words between us. I was also drinking, I'd been drinking too much myself. I thought . . . I don't know what I thought. We were both drunk. He slapped me and I slapped him back, the first time I ever hit him. His second slap was so hard my ears rang. It made me wild enough to try to knee him. He grabbed me, threw me on the floor, started yelling and kicking me. Half a dozen kicks in the side and hips."

"Hard enough to break two of your ribs."

"The last kick . . . I think I screamed before I passed out." Her voice was brittle, without emotion. She was like a sponge that had had all moisture wrung out of it and been left to dessicate, curl inward at the edges until it was little more than compressed dust. "When I woke up I was in his car, he'd carried me out and was driving me to the hospital. Crying the whole way, telling me how sorry he was, how much he loved me and that he'd never hurt me again."

"And after Dr. Caslon treated you, he talked to Eb and told him he'd better get counseling and gave him Richard Disney's name."

"Yes. He would've agreed to anything that night."

"Including you paying the hospital bill. The records are in your name."

"He had no choice then."

"Not until Sunday night, when he caught the thief at the O'Hanlon Brothers warehouse. Instead of turning him in, he extorted five hundred dollars from him. Received the full amount the next night, deposited it in his account Tuesday morning."

"Is that how he got the money? I knew it had to be something like that. He said he borrowed it, but I didn't believe him."

"The check he wrote was to you," I said. "To pay you back for the hospital bill."

"Yes."

"What'd you do with it?"

"Tore it up and threw the pieces in his face. A mistake . . . but I couldn't stand to take dirty money from him."

"When did that happen?"

"Tuesday evening, after I came home from work."

And later Eberhardt had gone back to Bolt Street. Not to

stake out the warehouse; not to gouge any more wages out of T. K. O'Hanlon under false pretenses. Because he'd picked it as his dying place. Gone too far finally, so far he couldn't come back. *I've had enough. I can't keep hurting anymore.* Himself or Bobbie Jean. And the trigger wasn't one thing but a chain reaction: him breaking her ribs, her having to pay the hospital bill, him sinking low enough to shake down Danny Forbes, and the last link, her tearing up his check and flinging the pieces in his face. *You won't believe this Bobbie Jean but I love you.*

"Wednesday A.M.," I said. "Tell me what happened."

"He died," she said.

"But not alone."

"No. Not alone."

A UPS van went rumbling by on the street. A couple of houses away, two boys—home for lunch or playing hooky—began yelling and performing loops and wheelies on their racing bikes. I listened to them while I watched Bobbie Jean, waiting for her to go on. But she just sat there in that gone-away posture, for so long that I had to prod her with words like barbs. Making them into a question because this was the part I wasn't sure of, the part I hoped I was wrong about.

"Did he kill himself, or did you do it?"

She heard me because she made a sound in her throat, low and inarticulate. But she didn't answer.

"Bobbie Jean. Did you kill Eb?"

"No," she said. "Yes," she said.

"Which is it?"

"I don't know."

"Don't play games with me."

"I'm not. I swear I don't know. You'll have to tell me."

"How can I tell you? I wasn't there."

Mutely she shook her head.

"He called you at two-forty that morning," I said. "On his cell phone." The last call of his life. And the record of it—to his home number, along with the exact time—right there on the final Cellular One bill, staring me in the face every time I looked at it.

"Yes."

"To say good-bye? Or was he still on the fence and wanted to be talked out of it?" One or both of the reasons he'd called me the week before, maybe. But more likely he'd been bitter and vindictive enough to want to lay a little of the blame on me. Leave me a legacy of hurt.

"Neither one. Help, my help."

"Make sense, Bobbie Jean."

"I'm trying to. I've been trying to make sense of what happened ever since that night."

"What did he say when he called?"

"He was drunk. So drunk I could scarcely understand him. He said he was going to kill himself, that he'd been thinking about it a long time and it was the only way. He said he'd been sitting there for an hour with the gun in his hand. He said he . . . needed me."

"Needed you. Meaning what?"

"He wanted me to drive down there. Right away."

"The alley, Bolt Street."

"Yes."

"And you went."

"Yes."

"Why? You could've called nine-eleven instead. Or Rivera or Joe . . . somebody."

"I was afraid if anyone but me showed up, he'd go ahead and do it. I believed I could talk him out of it. I wasn't thinking clearly, I'd been asleep and I was groggy and scared . . . I crawled into my car and drove down there, that's all."

"And when you got there?"

"He was sitting behind the wheel with the gun in his hand, just as he'd said. Spilled liquor and vomit all over him. He started to cry when I got in. He said he wanted to die. Couldn't stand to go on or to hurt me anymore. Said he'd written a note, it was in the glove compartment, and he'd been trying to finish the job ever since. Said he'd had the gun in his mouth a dozen times but he couldn't make himself eat it. 'I can't squeeze the trigger, Bobbie Jean, I can't make myself eat it.' His exact words."

Don't be surprised if you hear I ate my gun. And most handgun suicides by cops and ex-cops did go that way—barrel in the mouth, squeeze the trigger. A chest shot wasn't Eberhardt's way, the hard-line retired cop's way. It had never seemed quite right to me, despite Jack Logan's arguments. *Join me for a midnight snack? Let's eat.* Lodged in my subconscious and manifested in the recurring dream.

I knew what Bobbie Jean would say next. And waiting for it, I was cold all over and filled with emotion like a viscous fluid clogging my chest, making it difficult to breathe.

"He begged me to help him," she said. "I told him no. I tried to talk him into giving me the gun, coming home with me, but he wouldn't listen or he was too drunk to listen. He drank what was left in his bottle, threw it on the floor and cried and begged some more. I kept saying no and then, real foolish, I made a grab for the gun. He turned ugly. Laid the muzzle against my temple and said he'd kill me first, kill me sure if I didn't help him. He meant it. Dark in the car, I couldn't see his eyes, but I heard the truth in his voice. He'd've shot me if that was what it took to shoot himself. That's how much he wanted to die."

"You had no choice," I said thickly. "No other choice."

"I didn't see that I had. Maybe if . . . oh Lord, I don't

know. I was so scared and he'd made me hate him for everything he'd done to me, to himself—I wanted him dead right then as much as he wanted it. He put that gun in his mouth again and I let him take my hand and fold it over his hand, my finger over his finger on the trigger, and he mumbled 'Squeeze, squeeze' but I couldn't. In my mind I saw his head exploding and I couldn't do it, not that way. 'Not that way, Eb,' I said, we were both bawling by then, and he took the barrel out of his mouth and pressed it against his chest, his hand and mine, and said 'Squeeze' and I couldn't and he said 'Do it, please, for both of us, squeeze' and I squeezed . . ."

"Jesus, Bobbie Jean."

"The shot was so loud . . . I jumped and I think I screamed. But after that, it's crazy but I was real calm. Drug-calm, you know? As if I'd had a shot of something. I went from his car into mine and drove home just as if nothing'd happened. It wasn't until I was in the house that it came over me he was actually dead and I'd helped him die. For a long time I was hysterical. But by daylight, when the police called and said he'd been found, I was calm again. I thought I could tell them, but I couldn't. I thought: I've been through enough, I can't go through anymore. But I'm still going through it, over and over. That kind of thing just tears you up inside. And the worst of it is, I don't even know if I murdered him or not. Did I?"

"No," I said. "He murdered himself."

Her dark, dry, haunted eyes searched mine—the kind of look a supplicant might give to a priest. "You don't hate me?"

"I don't hate you."

"Sometimes I hate myself."

"You shouldn't. Him, if anybody."

"Funny, but I don't hate Eb. Not anymore."

Me neither, I thought. Maybe I never did. Maybe all along I was enraged at him for being sick, disappointed in him for being weak and flawed and culpable. And maybe I'd wanted to hang on to some of my belief in the old Eberhardt, the fantasy Eberhardt, even though I knew better. Some illusions die harder than others, and the ones closest to your own soul the hardest of all.

I said, "Look at it this way, Bobbie Jean. He felt he'd rather be dead than hurt you any more—and that's a form of love, isn't it? Bitter and twisted, but still love. So is what you did for him. An act of love as much as any other kind."

"It'd be a comfort to really believe that."

"Better than carrying the weight of him on your shoulders as long as you live."

"Someday," she said. "Someday."

The energy-high kids rocketed by on their bikes, yelling. A woman being half dragged by a standard poodle appeared on the sidewalk, stopped when the poodle stopped, and looked on with benign obliviousness as the dog lifted its leg and peed all over one of the Hoyts' yew trees.

"What happens now?" Bobbie Jean asked.

"Now?"

"You, me. Where do we go from here?"

"You go to work; it's almost one o'clock. And I drive back to the city and do the same."

"You know what I mean."

"No, I don't know. The fact is, I haven't seen or talked to you since last week. Any conversation we might've had after that is strictly imaginary."

The haunted eyes probed my face again in that seeking-sinner way. Her mouth opened slightly; her throat worked.

"Don't say it, don't say anything. Whatever it is I couldn't hear it because I'm not here." I pushed off the railing, leaned down and kissed the papery skin of her cheek. "Forgive yourself, Bobbie Jean. I already have."

And I said good-bye for the last time and left her sitting there and walked out of the rest of her life.

22

I TOLD KERRY THAT NIGHT OVER dinner. All of it, every detail. She had as much right to know the truth as I did. We'd had secrets from each other once, before our marriage, but not since and not ever again. Anything, everything that mattered to one of us now belonged to the other.

Kerry, yes, but nobody else. Our secret and Bobbie Jean's to the grave.

She took it as I expected she would: shock, bewilderment, sadness, understanding. "My God, that poor woman. What she must've gone through."

"Six kinds of hell and still burning," I said. "So you think I did the right thing? Not turning her in?"

"Yes."

"Letting her get away with a crime."

"I suppose so, but— Oh."

"Sondra Nelson and Gail Kendall, that's right. Nelson went through the same kind of hell, and for a much longer time, and she's still burning, too. So is Kendall after nine years."

"But Bobbie Jean didn't murder Eberhardt."

"Technically, no. But she did help him kill himself and then hid the fact. Assisted suicide is a serious offense in California, Kerry. Just about as serious as second-degree homicide."

"Which means you've decided. You're going to let Nelson and Kendall get away with their murder."

"I *have to*, now. How can I do anything else? I'd be the most despicable kind of hypocrite if I let a guilty friend off the hook and gaffed a couple of poor strangers. The cases are too similar, legally and morally and in every other way. You can see that, can't you?"

"Yes, I can see it."

"But you still don't approve?"

"I didn't say that. Part of me keeps balking at the idea, but another part . . ." She sighed and shook her head. "It's all so damn complicated."

"And the suffering makes it more so."

"You think any of them will ever find peace again?"

"I hope so. They wouldn't if they had to go through due process, that's for sure. Besides, if it happens I am wrong to be playing God this way, I'll answer for it some day."

"So will they."

"Right. One thing for sure: Eberhardt and Ira Erskine already have."

She was quiet for a time. Then, "I really don't know you as well as I thought I did," as if she were a little nonplussed by the admission. "Either that, or you keep changing in ways I'm not sure I understand."

"Do I seem that different to you?"

"Right now, yes."

"Maybe I am. But in only one way."

"Which way?"

"I'm like the kid who comes to realize Santa Claus and the Easter Bunny are a couple of big-time frauds. After nearly sixty years I've grown up. I don't have any more illusions, pretty or otherwise. I'll never have another as long as I live."